KER DUKEY & K WEBSTER

Daddy Me
Copyright © 2019 Ker Dukey
Copyright © 2019 K Webster

Cover Design: All by Design
Photo: Adobe Stock
Editor: Emily A. Lawrence
Formatting: Champagne Book Design

ALL RIGHTS RESERVED. This book contains material protected under International and Federal Copyright Laws and Treaties. Any unauthorized reprint or use of this material is prohibited. No part of this book may be reproduced or transmitted in any form or by any means, electronic or mechanical, including photocopying, recording, or by an information and retrieval system without express written permission from the Author/Publisher.

This is a work of fiction. Names, characters, places, and incidents either are the product of the author's imagination or are used fictitiously, and any resemblance to actual persons, living or dead, business establishments, events, or locales is entirely coincidental.

From international bestselling authors, **Ker Dukey and K Webster** *comes a **fast-paced**, hot, **instalove** standalone **lunchtime read** from their KKinky Reads collection!*

Dreams are supposed to be encouraged.
Not mine.
My brother likes to keep me on a tight leash, tethered to an unexceptional life.
But when Ronan Hayes walks into our family-owned bar, he opens my cage and offers me freedom.

Ronan wants to give me the world.
A chance to take flight and soar.
He sees something special in me, and I want nothing more than to be that for him.
Special.

He's my dream maker.
My shot. My hope. My everything.

Ronan craves to take care of me.
A protector. A confidant. A provider. A lover.
He wants to daddy me.
And I want to let him.

*This is a steamy, kinky romance sure to make you blush! A perfect combination of sweet and sexy you can **devour in one sitting**! You'll get a **happy ending** that'll make you swoon!*

This is not a dark romance.

BOOKS BY
KER DUKEY

Empathy Series:
Empathy
Desolate
Vacant—Novella
Deadly—Novella

The Broken Series:
The Broken
The Broken Parts of Us
The Broken Tethers That Bind Us—Novella
The Broken Forever—Novella

The Men by Numbers Series:
Ten
Six

Drawn to You Duet:
Drawn to You
Lines Drawn

Standalone Novels:
My Soul Keeper
Lost
I See You
The Beats in Rift
Devil

Co-Written with D. Sidebottom

The Deception Series:
FaCade
Cadence

Beneath Innocence—Novella

The Lilith's Army MC Series:
Taking Avery
Finding Rhiannon
Coming Home TBA

Co-Written with K Webster

The Pretty Little Dolls Series:
Pretty Stolen Dolls
Pretty Lost Dolls
Pretty New Doll
Pretty Broken Dolls

The V Games Series:
Vlad
Ven
Vas

KKinky Reads Collection:
Share Me
Choke Me
Daddy Me

Joint Series

Four Fathers Series:
Blackstone by J.D. Hollyfield
Kingston by Dani René
Pearson by K Webster
Wheeler by Ker Dukey

Four Sons Series:
Nixon by Ker Dukey
Hayden by J.D Hollyfield
Brock by Dani René
Camden by K Webster

The Elite Seven Series:
Lust—Ker Dukey
Pride—J.D. Hollyfield
Wrath—Claire C. Riley
Envy—M.N.Forgy
Gluttony—K Webster
Sloth—Giana Darling
Greed—Ker Dukey & K Webster

BOOKS BY
K WEBSTER

Psychological Romance Standalones:
My Torin
Whispers and the Roars
Cold Cole Heart
Blue Hill Blood

Romantic Suspense Standalones:
Dirty Ugly Toy
El Malo
Notice
Sweet Jayne
The Road Back to Us
Surviving Harley
Love and Law
Moth to a Flame
Erased

Extremely Forbidden Romance Standalones:
The Wild
Hale
Like Dragonflies

Taboo Treats:
Bad Bad Bad
Coach Long
Ex-Rated Attraction
Mr. Blakely
Easton
Crybaby
Lawn Boys
Malfeasance
Renner's Rules
The Glue
Dane
Enzo
Red Hot Winter

KKinky Reads Collection:
Share Me
Choke Me
Daddy Me

Contemporary Romance Standalones:
The Day She Cried
Untimely You
Heath
Sundays are for Hangovers
A Merry Christmas with Judy
Zeke's Eden
Schooled by a Senior
Give Me Yesterday
Sunshine and the Stalker
Bidding for Keeps
B-Sides and Rarities

Paranormal Romance Standalones:
Apartment 2B
Running Free
Mad Sea

War & Peace Series:
This is War, Baby (Book 1)
This is Love, Baby (Book 2)
This Isn't Over, Baby (Book 3)
This Isn't You, Baby (Book 4)
This is Me, Baby (Book 5)
This Isn't Fair, Baby (Book 6)
This is the End, Baby (Book 7—a novella)

Lost Planet Series:
The Forgotten Commander (Book 1)
The Vanished Specialist (Book 2)

2 Lovers Series:
Text 2 Lovers (Book 1)
Hate 2 Lovers (Book 2)
Thieves 2 Lovers (Book 3)

Pretty Little Dolls Series:
Pretty Stolen Dolls (Book 1)
Pretty Lost Dolls (Book 2)
Pretty New Doll (Book 3)
Pretty Broken Dolls (Book 4)

The V Games Series:
Vlad (Book 1)
Ven (Book 2)
Vas (Book 3)

Four Fathers Books:
Pearson

Four Sons Books:
Camden

Elite Seven Books:
Gluttony

Not Safe for Amazon Books:
The Wild
Hale
Bad Bad Bad
This is War, Baby
Like Dragonflies

The Breaking the Rules Series:
Broken (Book 1)
Wrong (Book 2)
Scarred (Book 3)
Mistake (Book 4)
Crushed (Book 5—a novella)

The Vegas Aces Series:
Rock Country (Book 1)
Rock Heart (Book 2)
Rock Bottom (Book 3)

The Becoming Her Series:
Becoming Lady Thomas (Book 1)
Becoming Countess Dumont (Book 2)
Becoming Mrs. Benedict (Book 3)

Alpha & Omega Duet:
Alpha & Omega (Book 1)
Omega & Love (Book 2)

"Worship me, Daddy."
"My dick is your throne, Princess."

For all the Daddy's girls.

PROLOGUE

Ronan

Twenty Years Old...

My stomach twists as I stare down at the check Mr. Warner has written for me.

I know it will cost me twice as much to pay it back, but it's worth it.

Mom's insurance was insufficient. Cancer will fucking do that. It's funny how insurance works—you pay and pay into it in the event you'll need it one day only to be told it won't cover what you really need. Because of the shitty system, she still needs financial help. Pride isn't something I can afford to have right now.

Giggles float into the kitchen right before a different female from last night saunters in wearing my kid brother's shirt.

Leaving little to the imagination, the thin fabric shows a clear outline of her tiny tits and hard nipples. Bruises and stains litter her upper thighs.

Do girls have no class these days?

Walking over to where I'm sitting, drinking a mug of coffee, she sidles up to my chair and leans her ass against the table as she looks down at me.

She smells of sex and cheap perfume.

"Mmm. Who are you?" she purrs, reaching down to steal some of my bacon from the plate in front of me.

Brat.

When I don't reply, she takes the mug from my hand and sips it. "I'm Briana." She grins behind the mug.

"I didn't ask," I grind out, taking back my coffee and putting it on the table.

"Your coffee sucks," she chirps, nonplussed at my attitude as she walks away. "How do you drink that stuff anyway? Do you have any alcohol?"

"You lack manners," I snap, stopping her in her tracks.

Snorting, she swings her body toward me and makes a gesture with her hands, holding them up in mock surrender, and laughs. "Ohhh, so sorry, Dad."

My hand whips out fast, grabbing her wrist and catching her off guard.

Tugging her body toward me, I throw her skinny ass over my lap. A screech leaves her lips, but she's too stunned to fight it. I tan her ass with the palm of my hand.

Thwap!

Thwap!

Thwap!

Shoving her to her feet, I narrow my gaze on her shocked face. Her jaw is unhinged—eyes wide. Fuck, I bet her panties are damp, too.

"Go get dressed. Tell my brother I'm leaving for the hospital. He can meet me there."

·····◇·····

This place reeks of misery and death.

Our mother is in her final hours of life. The battle has been long and tedious—hope given and then stripped away. Happy days are bleeding into long weeks of pain and suffering.

She was a good woman, a devoted mother. Losing her will be hard on both my brother and me. But to know she's no longer in a toxic hold of cancer's grasp will bring us a little peace.

I can only hope there's somewhere better she's going to.

"Did you spank my date?" my brother's voice croons, humor tinting his tone as he arrives and comes to stand beside me.

"She lacked manners, Ren," I state with a frown.

"She was a clinger. I didn't think I was going to be able to get rid of her. Your punishment did the job for me." He shoulder nudges me. "Thanks." He hands me a piece of paper with a number scribbled on it.

"What's this?"

"Her number. She asked me to give it to you."

Scrunching the paper up, I slip it into my pocket until I find a trashcan to throw it in.

"Gee, thanks." I grimace.

"No problem. You going in or going to stare at her through the window all day?"

I'm not ready.

"She looks peaceful," I mutter. "I don't want to disturb her."

She's left us. I can feel it.

"Did you get the money from William's father?" he asks, shoving his hands in his jeans pockets to stop the tremor of sorrow from being visible to me.

"I did."

"Enough?"

"Enough to pay Mom's final bills and enough left over to start our company."

"It's going to be a success, Ronan," he assures me. "It has to be."

Offering him a tight smile, I nod in agreement. "I don't know how to fail," I jest to lighten the mood and it works, making him scoff.

He knows it's true.

Failure isn't something I can allow.

We need a win.

"It's time, boys," the nurse informs us.

The pit in my stomach is back in full force. I grip my brother's shoulder, and for the last time, push open the door to Mom's room.

1

Ronan

Present—Twelve years later

Lighting a candle, I embrace the familiarity the scent brings and smile down at the photograph of my mother, brother, and me on a day trip to the beach before she got sick.

"Simpler times," Ren says, nudging me as he raises his near-empty bottle. "Twelve years and I still miss her."

I nod in agreement, words unnecessary at the moment.

Missing her will never leave us. Every year we spend this night together, lighting a candle in her memory. And every time it hurts.

"I have someone for you." He changes the

subject and walks over to plant his ass in the chair opposite my desk.

I pour myself a whiskey and pop the lid off another bottle of beer for him.

"Pray tell." I grin, handing him the bottle.

"An artist," he clarifies, taking the bottle and smirking. "Not whatever the fuck you have running through your mind."

Wouldn't be the first time he passed a woman my way.

"Don't leave me in suspense." I take the seat opposite him, watching as his eyes brighten with excitement.

"Young, fresh, untapped talent. No training, so she hasn't picked up bad advice or habits." He beams, enthusiasm brimming from him like an overexcited kid. I haven't seen him this happy in, well, forever. It's his girl. She's changed him.

"Her name's Sofina," he says from behind his bottle and takes a swig of his beer.

"Sofina." I let the name caress over my tongue.

I like it.

"She has a presence about her," he continues. "Captivates the room when she sings."

Listening to his excitement while he talks about a potential asset for the label should get me excited too, but there's a reason he's in my office talking about how amazing this girl Sofina is and not bringing her in to see me.

"So what's the catch?" I ask him, stopping him from carrying on his hard sell.

"She's perfect, Ronan. Like Halsey with a touch of that rock growl Pink has. I think she's marketable and will appeal to all genres."

"Again. What's the catch?" I narrow my eyes on him, and he rubs at his jaw and then grins.

There it is, asshole. The catch.

"Okay," he says with a sigh. "There's a brother, and he is a tad… What's the word?"

"Annoying?" I jest, raising a brow at him.

Giving me the finger, he leans back and pushes his hat from his head.

His hair is a mess, but that prick can pull it off. Running a hand through his mop of brown strands, he shrugs. "He's hard work, reluctant to have her let go of his apron strings."

"He's protective?" I ask, intrigued to know why it's the brother and not parents or a boyfriend who is giving him trouble.

Sometimes boyfriends don't like the idea of being left behind if an artist should take off. Other times a parent wants to hold onto power and paychecks. But an overprotective brother? This is a first for us.

"Possessive," Ren clarifies, licking his lips because he's fucking possessive too. Hell, we both are.

"He got a thing for her?" I frown and Ren screws up his pretty face.

"She's his sister, you fucking pervert." He shivers like the idea repulses him, but he's a kinky fucker, and there's not much that surprises me anymore. A brother wanting to fuck his sister isn't that unheard of, is it? Or maybe I *am* a fucking pervert. Either way, I haven't got time for drama.

"Artists come to us," I grumble. "We don't need to seek out girls who come with brother issues."

"Just daddy ones?" Ren quips with a smirk.

It's my turn to offer him the finger, but I don't. Instead, I click the computer on and begin looking over numbers for the last quarter.

I can see him glaring at me from the corner of my eye, but I wait him out. My little brother knows his stuff, and if this girl has caught his attention, then she will be as good as he says she is. But he doesn't need to know I'm keen to learn more. I'm still pissed about the last band he recently made me sign. The lead singer, Xavi, likes to be an asshole. My limit for assholes is maxed out. Dealing with some little girl's brother is beneath me, and the label we built from the ground up with blood, sweat, and miracles to make it a success.

Standing, he digs into his pocket and tosses his phone across the desk.

"She works at Ritz Russo's. Always gets a ten-minute slot on Friday nights. Check her out or don't, but if you don't and someone else scouts her, don't bitch to me." He taps the desk before pointing his finger in my direction. "I need to use the pisser, but I'll use the one in the hall. I know you hate people using your personal one, Princess."

I wait for him to leave the room before I pick up his phone and watch the video.

Dark hair falls around small shoulders, colors of purple and blue mixed into the brown strands. Heavy, dark makeup around her eyes masks her natural beauty. Those eyes—the color of sapphires, though—shine through the dark bar and pierce the veil of the camera screen.

There's no hum of chatter from the crowded bar as the intro music plays, which is unusual. It's hard to get the attention of everyone in a room, especially one filled with intoxicated people. But she has it. She holds them all in the palm of her hand.

She looks nervous, jittery even. Her eyes close and then her mouth opens.

Velvet tones resonate from the phone, making my dick harden.

There's a gravelly edge to her low notes that not a lot of female singers possess.

She's good. Really fucking good. With the right look and the proper marketing, she could be something special.

The door opens, and Ren saunters back in, holding his hand out for his phone.

"Well?"

"Leave the address for the club on your way out." I wave him off and go back to the computer, but I'm not concentrating on the numbers on the screen. No, I'm consumed with little Sofina's image playing through my mind on repeat.

2

Sofina

"Stock the fridge, clean the tables, and sweep the damn floor. Your college degree is going to waste and a dream to be a singer fading with every passing night," Rosy snaps, taking the bottles from my hand and stacking them in the fridge for me. "I don't know why you're still here. I thought the whole point of you going to college was so you weren't stuck here wasting your talents."

Rosy is the best damn bartender we have, but she's pushing forty, and recently found out she's pregnant, so she's decided to hang up her drink slinging days.

Fifteen years she's worked here. Hired by my father.

It's going to be tough when she leaves us. My brother is already freaking out about her replacement. Rosy is well liked and dependable. She's also a constant in our lives, which we tend not to have many of these days.

"The idea was that I use my degree for the business," I remind her with a sigh, leaning my butt against the bar, hating the thought of still being here when I'm forty.

She squats to pull out a crate of clean glasses from a bottom shelf.

"Rosy, please let me do it. You should be resting, not me."

Scoffing, she looks over her shoulder at me and rolls her eyes. "I'll be doing enough resting when I leave here. Why don't you go and warm up your pipes for later? Your brother isn't in for another hour."

My stomach jumps with the thought of having an hour with the mic before Lucca arrives, but the place still needs the tables wiped down.

"I should clean the tables," I utter, nibbling at my lip and wanting so bad to rebel. To do what I want for once.

"Sof, you're not Cinderella," she grumbles. "Your papa wouldn't have wanted you working in this damn bar. Hollie will be in soon, so she can clean tables. Now go make everyone happy and treat us to a song."

Looking around the bar, I notice there are only a handful of day drinkers occupying a couple of booths. The DJ isn't due in for another two hours and the equipment for open mic night is all set up and sitting there.

"Okay," I agree, grinning, before skipping happily over to the stage.

Standing on the small stage gives me a rush like nothing else. The nerves trickle through me every time my palms wrap around the mic, but as soon as my mouth opens to sing, everything fades. It's just the lyrics and me.

The bar disappears from view as my eyes close and I give myself over to the sound of my voice. Words flow, and my hips sway. I pull in all my stomach muscles and draw air into my lungs to hit the high notes. Suddenly, it's over, and the mic cuts out before I can finish.

My eyes spring open to find the intense blue eyes of my brother glaring up at me from the dance floor below.

Crap.

Disappointment blankets me and my

stomach drops from the look of anger and spite on his features.

"What the fuck are you doing? You know tonight's one of our busiest nights, and the tables need to be cleared." He fumes, the tattoos chasing up his neck coming to life with his anger.

"I just—"

"Just what? Just fucking around as usual. Get the tables cleared and then get behind the bar," he orders, storming off toward the bar.

I hate that he treats me like a child and runs my damn life.

He raised me when our father died unexpectedly of liver failure when I was fifteen, and he was only twenty-one.

He gave up school and his future to keep me from being put into foster care and took over the Ritz Russo's bar to stop Dad's legacy—*this place*—from going under. He blames me in a way for what he had to give up. He would never admit it, but I feel it in his tone—in his stares.

He's bitter…I can taste it.

Offering me a sad smile, Rosy places the cleaner and cloth on the bar for me to grab.

Fuck my life.

"I hate you!" I huff to my brother.

If he's going to treat me like a child, then I'll act like one.

"Yeah, remind me of that when you're sleeping under my roof tonight with a full belly from my stocked fridge," he spits out.

Placing my hands on my hips, I glower at him. "I pay my way, Lucca. You *make* me pay it."

"Nothing comes for free, Sofina," he grinds out, fixing a spirit bottle in place. "Dreams don't pay the bills."

Whatever. How the hell would he know?

Grabbing the cloth and spray, I stomp over to the first table and clean it even though it's already clean.

The bar music suddenly booms from the speakers, making me growl under my breath.

I could be the entertainment for this place if he weren't so damn uptight and a slave driver.

My feet carry me to the next table, but I stop short when I notice a pair of sleek men's dress shoes beneath it. I follow the pressed slacks up the man's long legs, my heart pounding wildly and free in my chest.

A solid torso is hidden beneath a slim-fitting suit jacket, expensive fabric in a vibrant, dark blue shade. Shirt and tie are bringing the whole show together in a well-packaged offering. But it's not the best part. Oh no, that face needs no help being noticed.

Hot damn.

A chiseled jawline lays the foundation for one beautiful face.

Glowing tanned skin, thick full lips, straight nose, and large mesmerizing dark eyes are welcoming me in. Topped off with a short dark haircut giving a no bullshit vibe.

I notice a pricey looking watch sitting on his wrist, twinkling under the low light, as he plays with a business card in his hand.

He has whiskey on the rocks, melting in a glass in front of him, but I still find myself asking, "Can I get you something?"

My pussy clenches when his tongue swipes out to wet his lips and his dark brown eyes dance with humor. He knows the effect he must have on women.

What the hell brought such a man to *this* bar?

Lifting his hand, he offers me the card. It's textured and has a masculine scent to it. *Interesting.*

I read the bold embossed letters.

Ronan Hayes, CEO of Harose Records

I turn it over to see phone numbers and an address.

My hand begins to shake as I look it over and then back at him. "Is this a joke?"

"I don't play games," his deep, baritone voice rumbles. "I want to hear you sing without the interruption."

His eyes hold mine with such intensity my lip trembles. It's almost intimidating being in his mere presence, yet I don't exactly want to leave it.

"Sofina!" Lucca barks, making me startle as embarrassment heats my flesh.

Mr. Hayes' eyes cut to my brother's and flare with something I can't identify, before coming back to mine and darkening.

Picking up his glass, he downs the contents, breaking an ice cube between his teeth as he does.

"The whiskey you serve here is weak. It lets this establishment down. Speak to the boss about improving his inventory." His words sound demanding.

Fidgeting, I shrug. "He's my brother, and he won't listen to me."

"Make him listen," he rumbles. "If you don't use your voice to be heard, what's the point in having one?"

"I…uh…"

"Are you going to sing for me, Sofina?" My name slips through his lips like silk on bare skin.

"When?" I squeak out, flustered and feeling a stirring so potent in my stomach it's making me dizzy.

"How often does opportunity come knocking?" he croons in a confident, rich tone. "Soon, Sofina. Very soon. Don't make me wait."

Damn, I've never been so enthralled by a man before, and I don't even know him.

"Sofina?" Lucca growls, coming up behind me. "Everything okay here?" My brother dominates my space and uses his *take no shit* voice to speak to Mr. Hayes.

"I was telling Sofina how authentic and beautiful her voice is," Mr. Hayes replies, making my entire bloodstream spike with adrenaline.

"Listen, pal," Lucca snarls. "She's not paid to entertain by the table. It's a bar, not a strip joint."

Shit, he's so fucking hostile all the time.

A throaty laugh barks from Mr. Hayes.

"It's certainly not. Strip joints have better whiskey," he quips, making my brother aware that he doesn't take bullshit from the likes of him.

Rising to his feet, a gasp almost slips past my lips from the sheer size of him dwarfing me. Slipping his hand into his pocket, he pulls out a money clip and drops a hundred-dollar bill on the table.

"For the brief, but satisfying entertainment," he says, smirking.

And then he's gone.

Dammit.

I turn on my heel to face my brother, fury pounding in my heart like a war drum.

"Do you know who the hell that was?" I screech, overcome with anger.

"An arrogant prick," he snorts, walking away from me.

"Lucca," I bark out, chasing after him. "That was Ronan Hayes from Harose Records. The fucking CEO of the Harose record label was here in your bar."

"Our bar and so?" he scoffs, like it's not the most incredible thing to ever happen to me.

"So?! So, that's insane. The odds of that happening are—"

"Are what? Because I don't see the big deal. He was an asshole."

"No, Lucca, you were the asshole. You can't treat paying customers like shit," I bark, following him across the bar.

"He was interested in your tits, Sof, not your vocal cords."

"They are nice tits." Hollie winks over at me, slipping off her jacket. Her arms are decorated in an array of colored tattoos. Pink mermaid hair is gathered down her back in a loose braid and the sides of her head are shaved. Her curvy figure is squeezed into a leather skirt and a tight tee ripped up the sides and across the chest. Pink Doc Martens finishes the ensemble. I wish I had her confidence.

"Can you stop fucking hitting on my baby sister?" Lucca demands scornfully. "I have enough of it from the customers."

"She's cute, Lucca," Hollie says with a sweet grin. "It's going to happen, so best get used to it."

"Why do you always focus on anything but my singing? Why do you assume he didn't simply like my sound?" I bring him back to what's important.

Folding his arms over his chest, he stops fucking around behind the bar to look at me for a second.

"He wasn't here long enough to hear your sound, Sof." His tone softens slightly. "I'm sorry, sis, but do you know how many fucking singers that guy will see come through his doors? How many pretty, little dreamers like you there are?"

"Lucca, that's enough," Rosy chides. "She's special, and the one person she needs to hear that from is you."

Throwing his hand up in the air, he narrows his eyes on Rosy.

"She doesn't need me filling her head with that shit when she has you doing it for me. It won't lead anywhere but disappointment. She needs to live in the real world, not this fantasy one in her damn head."

"Fuck you, Lucca, I'm taking my break," I snap, throwing the cloth at him and placing the cleaner down on the bar.

"Where the fuck are you going?"

"Out," I snap.

So I'm a dreamer. I'd rather be that than a bitter bastard.

3

Ronan

Sofina was so much more in the flesh than I expected her to be. The video Ren took of her didn't do her justice.

My mind conjures up the thoughts of her. Her petite and tight body has the perfect amount of curves and meat to make any man want to take a bite. Plump lips, juicy and seductive, draw you in and hold you hostage to the thoughts of what you want her to do with them.

Her expression of passion when she loses herself to the lyrics is intoxicating to watch.

My thoughts drift to her eyes, expressive and bright blue, curious and pure, exploring my face when she came over to my table.

I'd been sitting there all of fifteen minutes, but I knew from the first second of seeing her, I had to have her.

"Do you see what I mean?" Starla pouts, pointing to a page in her booklet that she created as part of her final course work for her class.

"The formatting is wrong," I say with a nod.

She wriggles in my lap and nuzzles her face against my chest. "Yes, and he won't fix it for me. He said it's what I asked for."

Taking the book from her, I close it and place it on my desk, allowing her the comfort she seeks. Starla and I have an understanding that's soon coming to an end.

"I'll have my people fix it for you," I tell her, stroking her hair and kissing the top of her head.

"I'm going to miss you when I go back home," she coos.

I hate that I'm distracted by thoughts of another woman with her in my lap. She deserves my attention when it's our time together.

My phone line shrills, but before I can pick it up, my office door bursts open, shocking both Starla and me.

A wide-eyed Sofina tumbles inside, flustered and out of breath.

"I'm sorry. She wasn't going to allow me in and I had to see you…" She stumbles over her words before her eyes take in Starla on my lap. "Oh crap. Sorry, I…" She turns around like she caught us in a state of undress.

My secretary, Eve, appears a couple of seconds later with a thin-lipped scowl on her face.

"I've called security. I'm so sorry, Mr. Hayes. She wouldn't listen when I told her she needs an appointment. I had no idea she was going to take off running, sir."

Tapping Starla's ass, urging her to stand, I nod to Eve. "It's okay. Leave us."

"Sir." She nods.

"Starla, I'll speak with you later. Be a good girl and close the door on your way out."

Without a word, Starla leaves us, closing the door behind her.

"Sofina." I say her name, demanding her attention without speaking the instruction.

She turns, her sheepish eyes scanning over my form.

"I blew it, right? I just needed to come and show you that I know opportunities like this come around once in a lifetime…"

Getting to my feet, I stalk over to where she

stands babbling, and I hold a finger to her heavily painted mouth.

"Shhhh."

Her gulp is audible, and a smile tilts my lips when she leans into my finger, pushing the flesh of her lips against the ridges there. It's not my usual way of conducting business, but damn, this girl is special.

"What you did was very rude. Poor Eve isn't built for chasing naughty little girls around," I admonish playfully, despite the hunger to discipline her.

Her body vibrates. She's ready to combust like a wound up jack in a box. I bet she's never had an orgasm that she hasn't induced herself.

"I'm sorry," she whispers. Her tongue purposely flicks out to taste my skin.

Fuck!

Hearing her apology and sensing her arousal is making me hard as stone.

I stroke my finger down her mouth as I move it away, making the bottom lip drag down and ping back into place as I do.

"I want to please you," she breathes, heavy-lidded eyes looking up at me through thick over-painted lashes.

Well, fuck.

"With my singing," she quickly adds.

I smirk, loving how flustered she is.

"So sing," I tell her, moving away from her before I lose my control and punish her for bursting in here like a madwoman.

I grab a tissue and remove her lipstick from my finger.

"I didn't prepare anything," she utters, frowning.

"Well, you should have thought about that before bursting in here asking for a shot to please me." I quirk a brow, folding my arms over my chest. I lean against my desk, crossing my feet at the ankle, watching what she'll do next.

"Okay," she says, nodding and shaking her arms out as she prepares herself. It's fucking cute as hell. And then she begins belting out lyrics with no warm-up, hitting every note and transforming us from my office to an intimate concert for two.

She's animated when she performs, but in the right way. Real, raw emotion. She believes in the words she's singing—the story she's telling her audience. She's sensational and so beautiful to watch.

I'm lost to her when she finally speaks, breaking the spell she's cast over me.

"Was that okay or should I do another?"

Striding over to her, I take her wrist and guide her over to my private bathroom. I wait for her to question me, but she doesn't. Instead, she allows me to take her inside and face her toward the mirror with me at her back towering over her small body.

Turning on the faucet, I take a fresh towel and dip it under the water flow. Taking her chin between my forefinger and thumb, I wash her face, removing the makeup she doesn't need. Her eyes never leave mine as she watches me through the mirror.

"Look at your face. Why would you hide such beauty beneath makeup?" I question, admiring the creamy skin, naturally tinted rose lips, and blue almond-shaped eyes that could bring a man to his knees in worship.

"It's a mask, I suppose," she answers, but her tone is unsure like she's asking the question rather than solving one.

Releasing her jaw, I work at removing the feathers in an array of colors from her hair and push her own dark strands over her shoulders when I'm done.

"You don't need to wear masks, Sofina. Just be you. You're magnificent."

Her chest rises and falls rapidly as she roams my face in the mirror. Her pouty, fat lips are parting with need. I've never had such intense, immediate chemistry with a woman before. But there's this pulsing need like a magnetic pull inside me, anchoring me to her.

"I'll offer you a recording contract today if you're ready for it," I tell her, making her eyes expand.

She spins to face me, a small hand covering her mouth.

"You have to be ready to take your opportunity, though," I tell her firmly. "To become who you're destined to be."

"I'm ready." She nods rapidly, tears filling her eyes, making them shine even brighter.

"Good. I'll get a contract written up."

Because I'm ready, too.

4

Sofina

After he takes my phone and inputs his number, he walks over to his safe on the wall behind his desk. I'm frozen in place as I stare at his perfect form. Tall, built, handsome. Every girl's wet dream.

Focus, Sof.

A man like him doesn't get with a girl like you.

He's refined, successful, and drips with masculinity.

I'm a girl who wears makeup to pretend she's someone better than she is.

Behind the makeup and the mask he wants me to stop hiding behind, I'm just Sofina Russo. A glorified bartender.

I need not get caught up in this fairy tale feel.

He's not a charming prince and I'm certainly no princess.

Looking down at the wad of cash Mr. Hayes places in my palm, I furrow my brows. "What is this?"

It's more money than I can make in a year—hell, two.

"Let's call it an advance," he rumbles. "I want you to go shopping. Find your true style. No mask, Sofina. Show me and the world who you truly are."

Okay, so maybe he's a little charming and a little prince like.

He curls his fist over mine, sending currents of excitement shooting through me at his touch, and places my handful of cash against my chest. I wonder if he can feel the way my heart is hammering against my ribcage. His lips lift in a gentle, encouraging smile.

"Have fun. Spoil yourself and learn about the real you."

"I can't accept this," I murmur, heat burning up my neck.

He lifts a brow. "You can and you will." His tone brokers no room for argument.

"Thank you." My voice is soft and breathy. I don't even sound like myself.

"You're welcome." His dark eyes flicker with an emotion I don't quite know how to read. "We'll be in touch soon."

At his soft dismissal, I scurry from his office. The secretary gives me a go to hell look, but I ignore her. I'm too busy shoving a giant wad of money into my purse.

Thousands.

He gave me thousands like it was no big deal.

Pocket change to a man of his caliber, but to a girl who competes for her tips with three other bartenders, it's everything.

I wonder how many artists he has to do this with, strip them down to the bare, raw marrow underneath. My mind flips to the image of the girl who was sitting in his lap when I arrived. Maybe my brother is right, and I'll have to thank him for this money later down the line?

No.

No way.

Ronan of all people doesn't need to be a slimy jerk. He's too successful and rich and handsome to need to coerce women. Oh God, he's handsome. And he smelled divine. Masculine and powerful.

Shit, I'm so attracted to him.

But that's not why he gave me the money—because

he thinks I'm pretty and wants to make me his. No, it's an investment in his artist.

Holy hell, I'm going to be his artist.

My stomach roils, and a wave of nausea washes through me. That really happened. I open my purse once more and look in at the money to make sure I didn't fantasize the whole thing. Nope! Green bills, lots of them. It suddenly feels okay. Like I'm being awarded a small amount of pleasure in my life that's held nothing of the sort thus far.

In somewhat of a daze, I head straight for the bar. My break was over an hour ago, and Lucca will ride my ass for it. For the first time in a long time, I don't care.

·····◆·····

Three days I've had this money. I haven't been brave enough to spend it.

Running my hands through the dollar bills, I spread them out on the bed and lie on top of it, thinking about Mr. Hayes.

Every day I get myself off to thoughts of him to the point of soreness. He's consuming my mind and body, and he doesn't even know it. It's becoming an embarrassing obsession. Thankfully it's my dirty little secret and no one is none the wiser.

My fingers dance over my skin, teasing myself, making my heart skip as I reach into the vault of my mind for his image. Flicking my tongue out to wet my lips, my back arches from the mattress as I touch myself and fantasize about the way he gripped my face after marching me into his bathroom. Heat and hard muscle caging me in as he forced me to look into the mirror. My clit throbs as I circle it with the pad of my fingers.

"You don't need to wear masks, Sofina. Just be you. You're magnificent."

A gasp escapes my lips when my mind conjures up his words and whispers them back to me over and over.

I imagine him pushing me forward, my hands reaching out to brace against the sink. His eyes are heating as they watch me in the mirror, those giant palms siding down my neck, arms, hips, thighs, ripping away the clothing barriers until I'm bare before him. My stomach dips and warm pleasure teeters me on the edge of orgasm. I imagine his hard cock being released from his slacks and slapping down on my ass crack, the heaviness of it making my pussy drip with an appreciation of what's to come. His eyes never leave mine as my pussy pulsates, begging for his huge dick to plunge into me. My nipples ache with the need to be sucked on and tormented. His hands splay across my ass cheeks and spread them, teasing my tight butthole with the threat of penetration. My breathing is hitched and legs spread farther apart on the bed so I can push three fingers inside. I'm slick and swollen with just the thoughts of him. I'd probably buckle like an overfilled dam if he actually touched me.

"Yes, yes," I pant as a wave of euphoria ripples through me when my thoughts go to him moving down from my asshole and taking my pussy with one forceful jerk of his hips. I snap from my fantasy when my door bursts open.

"Sofina, did you take my…oh, Jesus Christ, Sof."

Pulling the covers over my body, I point to the door screaming, "Get the fuck out, Lucca."

"I'm sorry," he grumbles, covering his eyes as he turns back toward the door. "Just wanted my black Candlebox sweatshirt. Have you seen it?"

Seriously.

Brothers.

Mine's an asshole.

"Fuck off, Lucca," I snap before muttering, "I'm never coming out of my room again."

"Don't be dramatic," he bites back as he stomps away.

I listen for his footfalls to fade down the hall and scrub my hands over my face. Mortifying.

When I finally come downstairs, he's in the kitchen eating a bowl of cereal.

His eyes scan me over the lip of the bowl as he shovels spoonful after spoonful into his mouth like a starved teen. I spot his Candlebox sweatshirt crumpled up on one of the chairs and roll my eyes.

"You shouldn't barge into my room like that."

"Obviously. Don't want to see that shit again."

I flip him off.

"Was that money you were rolling around in?" he asks. When I don't answer, he puts down his bowl and folds his arms over his chest. "Where did you get that kind of money?" He walks over to where I'm standing and narrows his eyes on me. "Because I know you don't make those kinds of tips."

I reach down for his sweater and shove it into his chest. "It's none of your damn business. And stay out of my room."

"Did that record label prick give you that with talks of how special you are?" He smirks.

"Fuck you, Lucca. Why are you so against me

being more than a bartender? Is it because you're worried I'll leave you like everyone else has?"

His fingers grip my shoulders digging into the flesh, making me wince. "I gave up my entire life to come back here for you," he snarls. "We live in the real world, Sof, with bills to pay in order to keep a roof over our heads. I can't be filling your head with dreams, knowing at the end of the day you're going to end up right back here working Dad's bar like me."

Knocking his hands away, I shake my head. "Not me, Luc. It's going to be different for me."

Snorting, he shakes his head. "Yeah, that's what I said too, and then Dad drank himself to death and I had to come home and raise you, so you didn't end up in the system."

"Maybe it would have been better if I did," I lie, spitting venom.

He grits his teeth and a muscle ticks in his jaw. "Take that back."

"I gotta go, or I'll be late for work," I snap, waltzing out. "Can't have that. My boss is a real douchebag."

I hear his calls all the way to the end of the front yard, but I ignore every single one of them.

5

Ronan

Three days I've kept my distance. Three long days. It's unusual for someone to have such a hold on me, but there it is all the same. An aura in the air whenever I think of her, and it's a fucking lot.

Sofina.

Fuck, I can't get her plump lips out of my mind.

Me: I'm signing her.

My phone chirps with an incoming message from my brother.

Ren: Told you.

Confident little shit.

Eve jumps up from her desk as I walk through the lobby of our building.

"Oh, Mr. Hayes. I'm sorry to bother you first

thing, sir, but we had an irate man call saying some awful things." She's out of breath and clearly flustered from the ordeal.

Placing my hand on her arm, I usher her down the corridor to my office and pour her some water. "Take a breath, and when you're ready, tell me what the man said exactly."

·····◆·····

That arrogant little prick.

Sofina's asshole brother crossed a line today.

How fucking dare he think he can call the main desk and rant about me paying Sofina for things that never happened.

Pushing my foot down, I speed the entire way to their bar.

Fire rages in my gut as I swing the door open and step inside. It's dead. Not a soul in sight. A shuffling sound filters through the air from behind the bar, but I don't see anyone there. Marching toward the sound, I look over the chipped bar and frown. Sofina is on her knees, scrubbing the floor with a brush.

"What are you doing?" I bark, and she lets out a scream, her body jolting and knocking into the bucket of water with her knees that she's bent over, causing it to splash up and everywhere, including all over the front of her shirt.

"Oh my God! You scared the crap out of me." She gasps, holding a hand to her chest. She then attempts to wipe her wet splotched shirt, but only makes the fabric stick to her skin and highlight the mounds of her breasts.

Standing, she awkwardly holds the shirt out away from her body and looks around me at the door. "We're not open yet," she says before biting her lip.

"Why haven't you spent the money I gave you?" I ask her, placing my hands in my pockets, so I don't reach out and tear the fabric away and take her on the bar.

Not yet anyway.

Her eyes enlarge, and she shifts from foot to foot. "How do you know I haven't?"

She's adorable, and the anger that was burning bright in my veins moments before is now at a simmer.

"Your brother called my office. He found you with it."

A beautiful pink tinge blossoms up her neck and over her cheeks.

Gulping, she looks down at her feet. "What exactly did he say?"

Shit not worth repeating. Shit that made her sound like a whore and me some kind of pimp. Fuck him.

"Look at me, Sofina," I demand, and she inhales roughly when I say her name.

Her head tilts up to stare at me, her pupils expanding as she darts her gaze between my eyes and lips.

"Do I intimidate you?" I ask her, slipping my hand from my pockets and leaning them on the bar.

She shakes her head, dropping her hands from her wet shirt and breathing heavily.

"You excite me," she admits. Honest and brave. Her words make my cock grow thick and heavy in my slacks.

She's a fucking hot mess, her hair messily gathered on top of her head, wet soggy sweats and a T-shirt two sizes too big for her frame. And yet I've never been more attracted to a person in my life. A way that has less to do with her looks and more about how she makes me feel in her presence.

Aroused.

Protective.

Possessive and in control.

"You should take off those wet clothes before you get sick," I rumble.

There's silence, and then she reaches for the hem of her shirt and lifts it over her head, dropping it to the floor with a splat and staring at me as her chest heaves. Her full round tits in her bra jiggle in an enticing way.

Fuck. Fuck. Fuck.

Slipping my jacket off, I walk around the bar and step into her space. She's frozen like a deer in headlights, and it excites me more than I like to admit.

Bringing my body up close behind hers, I relish the heat of her bare flesh burning into my shirt. I could take her right here, a big *fuck you* to her brother. But I'm not the asshole he thinks I am. I could have any woman I want. I don't need to sign Sofina to get her in my bed or give her money. She would succumb to me willingly either way.

Draping my jacket over her shoulders, I lean down, stroking my fingers across her neck as I remove a stray strand to tuck behind her ear before I whisper, "I'll see you soon. Spend the money, sweet Sofina."

·····◆·····

I've not stroked my own cock in a long time, but here I am like a rampant teenager tugging at the fucking thing like it's going to produce a genie and give me three wishes.

Sofina.

Sofina.

Sofina.

After I left her, I came straight back to work and called Starla into my office to let her know I was ending things a little sooner than planned.

Our time together was over. She cried as I hugged her. Asked if I was sure. I gently told her it was me and not her. Cliché and a little tacky but necessary.

It's the truth.

It's a truth I warned her of in the beginning, which she understood and agreed to.

As long as we were in our relationship, I would take care of her. But that I would never date her long-term or marry her. I was very upfront. At the time, she was eager to comply with my rules. She was saving for school that I've now taken care of for her. She wanted the money and attention and praise. She wanted the mind-blowing sex.

And I gave it to her selfishly.

But I respect her too much to be fucking her all the while thinking of another.

It's unfair.

My phone lights up mid stroke, interrupting my efforts. I growl, shoving my cock back in my slacks and snatching up the phone. It's a picture message. Sofina is lying on a bed surrounded by money.

Fuck.

Two seconds later, a written message comes in.

Unknown Number: How do I know what my style is? You want me to spend all this money, but I don't know that I can. It's harder than you think.

I'm harder than she fucking thinks.

I add her name to the number and stroke my fingers over her image.

She's wearing a tank top and cotton pajama shorts.

I check my watch to see it's after nine. I should really head home, but instead, I hit call.

"Hello?"

"Are you not working tonight?" I enquire.

"No, I was in today, but it's Lucca's late shift tonight. I'm home…alone."

A deep laugh resonates from my chest.

"You shouldn't tell men you're home alone, sweet Sofina. It's a sure way to have uninvited guests stopping over."

"You wouldn't be uninvited," she breathes.

Goddamn, she takes me from zero to a hundred in a second. Every part of me buzzes and burns with need.

"You're playing with fire," I growl.

"*I'm* on fire," she whispers, her voice taking on a husky undertone.

"Sofina, are you being a bad girl?" I groan, releasing my cock once more and giving the tip a squeeze.

"Depends on what you classify as bad, Mr. Hayes."

Fuck.

"Tell me what you're doing right now."

"Lying on my bed." A soft sigh escapes her. "On the money you gave me."

"And?"

"And speaking to you…while I touch myself."

"Where are you touching yourself?"

"My breasts and now…"

Heavy breathing sounds make my cock strain for release. I'm so fucking hard I could burst.

"And now?" I prompt.

"Inside my shorts," she pants out.

"Say the words, Sofina. What are you touching?"

"My…my pussy."

Good girl. Shit, I didn't expect this from her.

There's a reason I'm so fucking attracted to her. It's because she craves my praise and approval, probably as much as I want to give it.

"Tell me what it feels like to touch yourself," I urge.

"Gooooood," she drawls out. "I'm wet and warm and tight, Mr. Hayes."

"You don't have to call me Mr. Hayes."

"What should I call you?"

"What do you want to call me?" I ask, tugging at my thick length. Cum beads at the tip, glistening as I slide the pad of my thumb over it. Up and down in firm strokes, imagining Sofina is rubbing at her cunt as I do.

"I don't know…Sir?" She laughs, and then her breath hitches. "What do your friends call you?"

Damn, I want it all from her, her words, her giggles, her voice, her orgasms.

"They call me Ronan," I grunt. "Or sir," I add with a grin.

"Are we friends?" she asks.

"Do you want to be?"

"So much so. Good friends. Really good friends." She cries out, "Oh God…"

"Some people call me that too," I tease.

"What does the girl from your office call you?"

"Eve, my receptionist?"

"No, the other one."

Ahhh, jealous little girl.

I know she means Starla, but I like to torment her.

"You really want to know?" I growl, jerking my cock harder, listening to her making beautiful little sounds down the line. I want to reach through it and lick every inch of her. I shouldn't still be here. I should be hunting her down like the animal I am and devour her. Feeling her coming undone with me inside her.

"Yes."

"Daddy."

A lot of girls balk at that name and say it's gross, but not all of them.

The good ones like it.

"Daddy," she cries out like the perfect little woman she is.

My cum spurts from me like creamy ribbon streams. "You're a good girl, Sofina."

6

Sofina

I find myself staring at the money stuffed back in my purse and biting my nails anxiously. How am I supposed to know what it is Ronan is expecting me to buy?

After last night, I feel like I'm floating on a cloud that might disperse at any minute. The money was given to me for a purpose, and I feel like if I don't do as he wishes, I'm a fraud in some way. I zip up my purse and go to my wardrobe, but pause when I reach for a black shirt.

Edgy. Dark. Heavy makeup.

He's right. I do hide. When I was growing up, I was obsessed with Adele. Her voice was majestic and she was classically beautiful—still is. Her voice stole the show, not her style or looks.

I drop my hand and look down at the vest top I'm wearing. It's gray, dull, boring. On a whim, I change into a navy dress that feels a little more airy and girly. I could use more outfits like this one.

Maybe a shopping spree is exactly what I need.

"I need you to take a shift today. Hollie is out sick," Lucca barks from the kitchen.

Ugh.

I swear, my brother has a radar anytime an inkling of happiness or excitement flitters through me. It's like he homes in on it and tries to squash it like it's a pesky bug.

"No," I tell him as I make my way into the kitchen. "It's my day off. I have plans."

"I'm not asking," he fumes, pouring a mug of coffee.

"No, Lucca. You can either ask nicely and sweeten the request, or you can find someone else."

"You're a fucking brat. You know that, right?" He slams the coffee mug down, making the brown liquid spill onto the counter. "Fine, you can have the stage for an hour."

My heart skips and my stomach flips. "Really?"

"I've never questioned your talent, Sofina. Only your expectations of an industry flooded with talented people willing to do shit to further themselves in it. It's a dog eat dog world out there."

"Maybe I'm a wolf," I tell him bravely. "Or one of the lucky ones who catches a break."

"Maybe," he says with a shrug, sipping from his mug. "But until you fly off to stardom, you have a job and work for me. And I need you to cover at the bar tonight."

"Fine," I concede. "I'll be there by eight."

"Seven," he barks.

Dick.

·····◆·····

The mall is bustling when I get there and I feel a little out of sorts wandering around alone trying not to feel like I have a bomb in my purse rather than a load of cash.

I see a shop I've always admired, but could never afford to go inside before.

Lucca loves window shopping, but for me, I always hated it. If I can't have those things, I don't want to see them. It's cruel.

Pushing inside, I discover it smells of expensive perfume and wealth inside. Gloss white floor shiny enough to reflect your image back at you holds racks of clothing more expensive than the average person's rent.

Yikes.

I bet Adele shops at places like this.

I bet Ronan does too.

Walking over to the formal section, I bite my lip, taking in all the pretty gowns. So many glitzy, sparkling dresses beg for my attention. Suddenly, I feel as though I'm a little girl once again, wanting to be a big music star.

The dresses are pricey, but my purse is heavy. For once, I give in. I try on all the beautiful dresses without any regard to the price tag with help of an elegant shop assistant. At first, she frowned at me and followed me around the store for the first few minutes until I opened my purse to get my phone out and my stack of cash flashed in her eyes. She was like the best friend I never had after that.

Eventually, I end up with a fitted, shimmery black number with long sleeves and an open back. It's classic and sexy. Within an hour, I've chosen jewelry and shoes to go with it.

One outfit.

I've come up with one outfit.

This is harder than I thought.

When I'm tired and think I may quit for the day, my phone buzzes.

Ronan: Did you buy anything yet?

My heart flutters thinking of seeing his name in my phone for the first time after he added it. My cheeks heat thinking of our call last night.

Me: I found a beautiful black dress, Mr. Hayes.

He replies back immediately.

Ronan: Mr. Hayes? You changed your mind about what to call me? And black? I thought we were steering away from the norm…

His admonishing tone through text makes me sit up straighter. I change his contact in my phone to Daddy and snap a picture of the fabric beneath the bag.

Me: Turns out, I was buying the wrong black all along. This black, I think you'll approve of.

Daddy: Good girl. Can't wait to see it on you.

My skin flushes at his praise. How is it this man gets inside of me so easily?

Daddy: Make sure to purchase some more casual things. And I'd love to take you to dinner. I have standing reservations at most of the restaurants in town. Dress nicely for those times.

I let out an unladylike snort.

Me: Sure thing, Dad.

As soon as I hit send, I worry he'll be offended. It's just that his bossiness had me feeling playful.

Daddy: That's Daddy to you, sweetheart. Don't sass me. I'd hate to have to redden that beautiful ass of yours.

Heat pools in my belly and I wonder if my cheeks are blazing red. What I do know is my panties are soaked and I should buy some new ones while I'm at it. Silk…lace…

Me: What do you prefer? Lace or silk?

My phone rings and his name pops up on the screen. I panic and drop the phone. It's different when I'm alone in my room to being at a store in front of people. His voice does things to me and I know it will be apparent for anyone who looks at me.

Daddy: Sweetness, answer the phone.

His command is sugary, but still that. A command. I find myself straightening and eager to please. What does this man do to me? This time, when he calls, I answer.

"Hello?" I say, my voice breathless.

"Your question was vague, Sof. Are we talking dresses or underwear?" he rumbles.

"Panties," I whisper as I pick up my things and head to the dressing room to get some privacy.

"Who will you be wearing them for?"

I freeze at his words. Does he want me to say him? Or…

"For me," I say after a beat of silence. His heavy breathing and words make me weak with need.

"That's a good answer," he praises. "This is all about you. Finding out what you want and like—and taking it."

Damn, I want him.

Can I go to him and *take* what I need?

"Mmmm…" I groan. My heart is racing in my chest. "I like the feel of silk against my skin. It's like a caress without even being touched. Yet, lace is sexy to look at."

"Lace can empower. Depends if you like to be in charge or if you want to let someone else have the control, to take what they like, and to own you." His deep voice slides through my veins like a drug, addicting me instantly.

I bite on my lip to keep from saying the word. In the end, I blurt it out anyway, eager to pull off the proverbial Band-Aid. "I want you to own me, Daddy."

His deep, rumbling chuckle echoes down the line. "Oh, I already do. Now be a good girl and get a mix of lace and silk."

"Don't forget the classic cotton for days I'm feeling virginal," I say with a girlish giggle.

"Where are you right now, Sofina?"

"In a changing room," I exhale, my pussy throbbing with need.

"I want you to slip out of your *virginal cotton panties* and stuff them in your purse," he instructs, making my entire body catch fire. "Tell me when you've done it."

I do as I'm told and feel the wet patch in my panties as I push them into my purse. "They're in my purse," I breathe.

"Good girl," he growls. "Good, good girl. Now get back to shopping. Later, I'll Facetime you so you can show me everything you bought."

Holy shit.

"You want me to shop with no underwear on?" I gasp.

"Yes. I want you to feel your arousal on your thighs. I want your pussy to ache and drip with need for me. I want you bare and ready to be taken at any moment."

My arousal is out of control and my thighs are already damp at the very thought of prancing around with no panties on and knowing he knows it.

For Daddy.

Heat burns across my flesh at the thought. This is silly! But so fucking hot, too.

"Okay."

"Okay, what?"

I choke down the whine of need, the desperate plea I want to cry out *come fuck me, please* and instead I say, "Okay, Daddy."

"Goodbye, beautiful." With those words, he hangs up the phone. He didn't seem at all flustered by our little exchange as I am. In fact, he seemed pleased with himself. Knowing I made that beautiful man happy is thrilling.

I'm riding on my high all the way from the mall to the bar. Wondering about what it is Ronan wants from me. He likes my voice. That much was evident. But all this other stuff? I thought, at first, he wanted to make me more sellable for his label. Nothing about our conversations thus far has been that simple, though. There's a connection between us. Real and sparking. I know I'm not imagining things.

Once inside the bar breakroom, I pull out the huge wad of money. I spent eleven hundred dollars today and barely scratched the surface. I'm scared to count it—to put a dollar amount on what he's given me.

"What the hell, Sofina? Did you rob a bank?" Rosy blurts, startling me.

I shove the money back into my purse and glance up at her guiltily. "What? No!"

Rosy, always quick to sniff out my lies, narrows her eyes at me. "Where'd the money come from then?"

"Tips," I squeak, shrugging my shoulder.

"Hmmm, not on my best day, even in my youth," she scoffs.

"Can we drop it?" I rush out. "I don't want my brother on my case."

"On your case for what?" Lucca says, coming into the back room.

Fucking great.

"About my money." I sigh, throwing my hands in the air, daring him to be a dick.

"I already saw the fucking money, Sof, remember? You were rolling around in it."

Oh God.

Rosy's eyebrows rise and she then ducks her head before waving goodbye, clearly not eager to be included in *that* conversation. She was supposed to quit this place already.

Anger surges through me. I never stand up to him. Maybe it's time I do.

"I went to see him," I blurt out, my voice only slightly shaking.

"Who?" he growls.

"Mr. Hayes. He wants to offer me a recording deal. He gave me the money to re-style myself."

Lucca's face nearly turns purple. "I knew it was him who gave you the money, Sof. I'm not fucking dumb. He already wants you to change who you are? And you think guys like him just hand over cash like that and want nothing in return?"

"It's my life, Lucca! And it's part of my offer. An advance." I lift my chin.

"He's a phony," he roars. "Recording labels don't pay cash! I can't believe you'd accept his word and not even talk it over with me!"

Tears burn at my eyes. "He's not a phony," I defend. "He gave me some money to buy some new things to wear. It's called being nice. You should try it sometime."

He snorts and his eyes turn cruel. "This is why you've always needed me. You're too blinded by the starlight to see the shadows creeping in. I'm your big brother, and now that Dad's gone, the one responsible for looking after you. People aren't nice. Not without wanting something nice in return. Hayes is a predator who preys on young, innocent hopefuls like you. I can see it from a mile away."

"Screw you," I choke out, hot tears running down my cheeks.

"*He* will," he tells me coldly. "After he gets what he wants, you'll be on your ass. And who will have to help you back to your feet?"

Not waiting for an answer, Lucca storms away from me. When he makes it to the doorway, he turns to glower at me.

"Tomorrow, you're returning that money. You'll distance yourself from him."

And then he's gone.

I slide to the floor, sobbing. For once, I want my brother to encourage me and be happy for me. But that's asking too much. It's like he thrives on holding me back.

My phone buzzes and I fish it from my purse.

Daddy: What time is your shift over?

I should end this thing like Lucca wants me to do. It would take out the tension between me and my brother. Life would go on as usual. And I'd drown in the misery that was my life before Ronan Hayes. If he didn't offer me a deal and wanted to take me out for a drink instead, would that make things better or worse?

Stubbornness burrows its way in my bones.

I don't want to give up this feeling making me feel alive for the first time in my life.

Lucca wants to treat me like a spoiled brat? Then I'll be one.

Me: Not soon enough.

He replies back immediately, sending a thrill running through me.

Daddy: What's wrong, sweetheart? Do you need your daddy to come rescue you?

The fact this handsome, nearly stranger cares about me more than my own brother is surprising. It makes me realize I've lived squashed under my brother's thumb for too long.

Me: I feel like I'm swimming in the deep end without a floatie.

Daddy: It's a good thing I won't let you drown.

I swipe away my tears and smile at the phone.

Daddy: I'm on my way.

My stomach does a flop in equal parts anxiety and excitement. Lucca won't let me leave. It's my shift and we don't have anyone to replace me.

Me: I don't think that's a good idea.

Daddy: I'm going to take a stab in the dark and guess that your brother is forbidding you

to associate with me. But your brother isn't in charge of you anymore. He's done a terrible job thus far. Broken your sweet little spirit. And I'd be a horrible daddy if I didn't come rescue my girl and set the record straight. You're mine now, sweetheart.

I gape at his text, my heart thundering in my chest.

Me: I'm not sure I can get away.

Daddy: I think what you meant to say was, "Yes, Daddy." See you soon.

"Yes, Daddy," I mutter, shocked at the way my skin seems to come alive.

Holy shit.

I feel like I've just opened Pandora's box.

I'm not sure what's about to come out, but I've never been so thrilled in all my life.

7

Ronan

I email the contract to Eve to have her print it off before I leave. The contract is generous in Sofina's favor. If Ren read through it, he'd make fun of me for being a pussy and giving her everything on a platter.

Generous royalty percentages.

Small fee to the label.

Creative liberties.

Basically, after barely knowing the girl, I've given her what most artists negotiate back and forth to get even a fraction of what I'm offering.

But that's not all I'm offering.

The moment I had Sofina in my office, the world narrowed its focus until all I saw was her. The beautiful girl hiding behind the wrong makeup, the wrong hair, and the wrong clothes. I'm going to help make her right. Teach her to blossom into the gorgeous flower I know she can be.

I need this contract signed and out of the way so it's not hovering over her decisions. The contract states she can't be dropped for the first five years of her contract. I've put Ren as her manager and given him all decision-making abilities about her career, so it's not part of what we have. I'm already in too deep to turn away from her now. It's fast but explosive between us. I've never wanted anything more than an arrangement before. And that was always fine.

Until things changed.

Perhaps I sensed it long ago. That someone would come along. Someone I'd never be able to ignore. Isn't that what everyone holds out for? Someone so alluring and wonderful that you can't deny it for a second the moment they walk into your life?

The moment I saw Sofina in that bar, I was smitten.

The moment she stormed into my office, I was turned on.

And the moment she belted out the most stunning music I'd ever heard, I knew she was mine.

I quickly check my phone while I wait for Eve to bring me the contract packet. Sofina hasn't texted me anymore. No, my girl is waiting for me to come rescue her from her brother. She doesn't have to say it or beg for me to do it. I can read it through her unspoken words. I'd seen it dancing in her eyes.

She needs me.

And I need her.

Something about her calls to my inner desire to own, mold, and hold that girl. She is a flame and I'm a motherfucking moth desperate for a chance to get burned by her. I need to stoke her fire. Show her what she's made of. What she can be.

The music. The stardom. Her career. That's all a given. It has nothing to do with what else I want from her. If she decides she's not into things with me and doesn't want me, then she'll have a nice recording contract with the best music label of this decade. I'll step aside.

But I know she wants more. She wants me just as bad. She feels it, this smolder between us waiting to turn into an inferno. She needs more.

She needs the opportunity and she needs someone to hold her hand as she makes her way there. Her brother should have been that encouraging force in her life. Instead, he chooses to shove her into a dark box and seal it shut. The bastard is crushing her delicate spirit.

Not anymore.

"Here you are, sir," Eve chirps, handing me the packet.

I give her a smile as I tuck it into my bag. "Thanks, Eve. How was Starla?"

She purses her lips. "Saddened that she would be leaving sooner than expected."

"How did she enjoy her parting gifts?"

"She took that a little better," she admits. "I mean, you gave her a car and padded her bank account. Who would be unhappy with that?"

I give her a nod. "Very well. Good night."

As I walk to my car, I smile knowing Starla will be okay. I spoiled her, yes, but she's more than a spoiled girl. Starla is smart and has drive. She'll go on to do great things. I hope the next man in her life doesn't undo all the hard work I put into her. I hope he cherishes her. Starla deserves it. I'm just not the man to give it to her anymore.

The drive over to Ritz Russo's is short and I'm nearly shaking with pent-up energy to see Sofina. This is why I had to pounce on her. She's a breath of fresh air. I hadn't realized I was only inhaling stagnant air this whole time until she blew into my life.

I park in the shitty parking lot and make my way into the bar. It's busy, but not horrible. I find Sofina behind the bar, her head bent down as she makes a drink. Her controlling brother is scowling at her, his jaw flexing.

What a fucking prick.

The desire to ram my fist through his face is strong, but I settle for meeting his gaze and giving him a smug look.

I'm here for your baby sister, man.

A vein in his forehead throbs to life, revealing his fury at seeing me. Unperturbed, I saunter toward him, extending my hand in greeting. He darts his gaze to the left, noticing a couple of patrons watching, and begrudgingly offers his hand to me. I shake it, meeting his firm grip with one of my own. He practically jerks his hand from my grip.

"What can I get you?" he growls.

My eyes slide over to Sofina and linger, before I meet his malevolent eyes. "I'll take something sweet. Something that gets you drunk from one taste. One of your favorites. What will you give me?"

His neck muscles twitch, making his tattoos seem to come alive. "Drop the fucking act," he snarls.

I hold up my hands, feigning innocence. "Just want a drink."

Turning on his heel, he storms off. My eyes meet Sofina's. Her cheeks darken to a beautiful rosy pink. It makes me wonder if her whole body turns that lovely shade when she's naked and beneath the touch of an experienced man. I walk over to the bar and sit down right in front of her.

"The contract is in the car," I tell her, smiling. "Don't tell my brother I gave you the world. He'd try to talk me out of it." I wink at her, loving the way she beams at me.

"I can't believe this is real," she says with a quick glance to make sure Lucca is out of earshot.

Reaching across the bar, I take her hand. "It's real. You're a star, Sof. It's time you start shining like one." My thumb runs across her soft skin. "But tonight…"

"Tonight, what?" her brother snarls, slamming down a tumbler of something dark.

"Lucca!" Sofina shrieks. "Stop!"

He turns her way, searing her with a nasty look that has her cowering. Fuck this guy. Fuck the way he tries to pin her down when she was meant to fucking fly.

"Tonight, she's coming home with me." I smirk at him.

"The hell she is," he roars, no longer caring about his patrons. "Get the fuck out of my bar, asshole."

I pick up the glass and drain it, my eyes locking on his. I set it down and shake my head. "Your sister needs a break from you. You've done enough damage for one lifetime."

My words wind him because he visibly flinches. Guilt flashes in his eyes before he hardens his stare once more. Turning from me, he glowers at Sofina.

"We're understaffed," he growls at her. "You're not leaving. So help me, Sof, if you leave, you can't come back."

Her eyes water and her bottom lip trembles. Later, I'll soothe away all her heartache.

"Lucca," she chokes out. "I do need a break. Not only from this damn place. But from you. You're smothering me."

His jaw clenches and he fists his hand. It makes me wonder if he's ever put his hands on her. If he has, and I find out, I'll bury this asshole myself.

"I'm your goddamn brother. He's what? Some suit you met for a week? Come the fuck on, Sof. Look at you. You're practically creaming your panties for whatever false promises this smarmy dickhead is offering you. Wake the fuck up. There is no contract. He wants to fuck you."

A girl walks past, and I tap her shoulder. She looks at me in confusion before a smile turns her lips up. "Yes?"

"How'd you like to make a thousand bucks tonight?" I ask, challenging her with a lifted brow.

Her mouth parts. "I'm no prostitute."

I fish out a grand from my pocket and hand it to her. "Help that guy out for the night." Then, I nod my head at the door, my eyes penetrating Sofina. "Let's go, sweetheart."

Lucca's face is turning more purple by the second. I expect Sofina to fret or stall, but she surprises me. She must be more eager to get away from her brother than I ever thought because she bolts to the back. A few seconds later, she returns with her purse. I slap down a hundred-dollar bill for my drink and then walk away, ignoring the hateful look directed my way.

Sofina rushes over to me and I take her hand. So small in mine. She's so desperate to be taken care of—truly taken care of. In a way her controlling brother never could.

I tug her outside and to my car. When I get to the passenger side door, I stop her by grabbing her hip and pressing her into the side of my car. Gently, I stroke her hair from her eyes—eyes she's left untouched by makeup, which pleases me.

"I'm so proud of you," I tell her, my gaze drinking up every pretty part of her face in the moonlight.

Her eyes widen and her mouth parts. "Why?"

"You stood up to him. You came with me. Where you belong."

She bites on her bottom lip, her brows scrunching together. "I don't know what I'm doing. If I'm making a mistake…or ruining my relationship with my brother."

I slide my palm to her delicate neck, loving the way her pulse beats erratically beneath my thumb. "Your relationship with your brother wasn't healthy. Maybe it needed to get ruined first before it could ever have any hope of being repaired."

Tears glisten in her eyes. "Maybe."

"This thing between us has nothing to do with music or the contract," I tell her, my eyes dropping to her plump, juicy lips. "If you walk away from me, you have a solid future. Understand?"

She nods rapidly.

"This thing is different and we'd be idiots not to allow it to happen," I rumble, leaning against her body so she can feel the effect she has on me. "Do you feel it too?"

"Y-Yes," she breathes.

"Yes, what?" I murmur, pressing a soft kiss to her perfect lips.

"Yes, Daddy."

"Good girl," I croon. "Good fucking girl. Now I'm going to take you home so I can properly reward you."

Her eyes close and I kiss her supple mouth deeply. She deserves a taste of what's coming. And it's coming all right.

I palm her ass cheek and grin against her lips. "Where're your panties, Sof?"

"In my purse," she exhales, melting into me.

Opening the car door, I pull away from her and nod for her to get in. Once she's inside, I grab her purse, unzipping it and taking out the underwear. Black cotton. I bring them to my nose, inhaling, and my dick jerks. Then I put them in my pocket and take my girl home.

8

Sofina

My heart is racing. Like a flock of birds are inside me, batting their wings against my ribcage. The entire drive is like a tension-filled hotbox.

"Your contract is in the glove compartment. Take it out and sign it," he demands. "Then put it back and part your thighs."

My gulp is audible. I open the compartment and pull out a thick envelope.

"Shouldn't I read it first?"

"Yes, but I can't touch your sweet pussy until it's signed." He grins, looking over at me. "I don't want there to be any confusion between us. The contract is a great fucking deal, Sofina, and it comes with no strings attached. Only your promise to work to the best of your ability as an artist."

I nod, my hands shaking. This is happening. A record deal.

"Whatever happens from here on out, your career is safe. I need you to understand that."

God. I'd take him over the damn deal if it came to it. I want him so badly I can hardly think.

"Pen?" I whisper, my voice raspy with need.

He lifts the arm of his seat, and there's a compartment with a notepad and pen. I reach for it and flick through the pages until I see a few tabs for my signature. I squiggle my name in all the appropriate places before shoving the contract back in the glove compartment and reaching for his hand.

He's warm to touch, masculine, a roughness that makes me squirm. I place his hand on my thigh and then part my knees.

His intake of breath empowers me, and I feel brazen and beautiful in the small confines of the car. I'm wearing a calf-length dress that's gathered up over my knees. The fabric ruffled and loose, allowing him entry to his destination.

When he skims his palm up my bare skin, a zap of energy hums through me.

The engine roars, the speed and powerful car vibrating the seats, adding to my need.

His descent is slow and torturous. I push my hips forward, urging him to hurry up, but he simply chuckles.

I blow out a breath and whine, "Touch me, please."

"Please, what?"

"Please, Daddy," I groan.

His tongue slips out to wet his lips, and I have to bite mine to stop from moaning. His fingers tease my slit, stroking at the wetness gathered there. When he pulls his hand away, I gasp in shock and sit up to gape at him.

He tastes the tips of his fingers and sighs. "You taste divine, sweetheart."

"I need more, please," I beg, squeezing my inner muscles to try and relieve myself of the need to come.

The car slows and he pins me with a devilish smirk. "We're home. I'm going to eat your tasty pussy in about two minutes. Be patient."

Oh, fuck.

We pull up to a large gate that opens on its own, leading up to a winding driveway. When we reach the top, a colossal house ten times the size of my own stands proud, surrounded by acres of land and lush landscaping illuminated by the moon and fancy lighting.

He's not only wealthy. He's rich, rich. Mega loaded.

Oh, God. What the hell is he doing with a girl like me?

As if sensing my self-doubt, he grips my hand and says, "This is just stuff, Sof. I didn't always have money, and one day you'll have all this too. Bought by you because of your talent."

When he puts it that way, I don't feel so bad.

He shuts off the car and we head inside. It's like nothing I've ever seen before. Well, only in movies. He drags me through the lobby into a huge kitchen. Before I can take any of it in, he grips my hips and lifts me onto the counter.

"Lean on your elbows, beautiful. I need a little taste."

I arch back and watch him push up my dress to admire my pussy.

He strokes a finger over the little bit of hair I keep there, and he grins. "I like this. Damn, you're pretty, sweetheart."

His words make me melt, but it's the way he says them that has me on fire. I believe his words. He truly likes what he sees.

Thank God.

I couldn't bear for him to back out now.

Hooking my feet on the edge, he pushes my thighs wide, and the cold air hits my warm lips as they part like a flower for his devouring.

"Fucking perfect. Be a good girl and ask me to eat your pussy, Sof."

He's trying to kill me.

"Please eat my pussy, Daddy," I choke out, ready to combust.

"So polite," he croons. "How can I refuse my good girl?" With that, he lowers his mouth onto me, kissing my clit before licking up the slit.

My head drops back, and I shudder from one touch. Tingles shimmer up my spine and shivers sprinkle goose bumps all over my flesh.

Curling his arms under my thighs, he palms my hips, gripping me to him.

Licks and kisses torment me in the most delicious of ways. He teases my dripping hole with his finger, dipping in shallow and swirling. Without warning, he sucks hard on my clit and plunges two fingers inside, crooking them in a come-hither motion, hitting me right in a spot that makes me cry out in pleasure.

The slight stubble on his chin grazes my thighs,

and it makes me even more turned on. His lips taste and devour, his tongue lapping like I'm made of ice cream. He inhales my scent and eats me out until I'm soaked with release and a quivering fucking mess.

My legs shake uncontrollably as his fingers fuck me and he flicks his hot, wet tongue over my clit nonstop. Heat pools in my stomach while my walls pulse and contract around him as an explosion of euphoria dances behind my eyes.

"I'm coming," I cry out, clutching my thighs closed, trapping his head. He doesn't stop his ministrations. His fingers thunder into me hard and fast as he sucks on my clit until a flood of release bursts from me, uncontained and raw, causing me to moan so loud it echoes around the room. My pussy leaks all over his fingers, coating him in my juices.

Before I can even catch my breath, he's dragging me down from the countertop to my feet. He smashes his lips to mine in a claiming kiss. I taste myself on his lips and groan with him as our tongues duel.

Pulling away roughly, he grips my dress around at the collar and tears it all the way down, sending buttons pinging to the floor, until it gapes open and slips off my shoulders onto the floor. He does the same thing with my bra, gripping it in two fists and snapping the fabric that tethers it together—pushing the material from my body. He studies my naked flesh with an intensity that makes me tremble.

"You're remarkable," he breathes. Leaning down, he takes nearly a full tit into his mouth, sucking and releasing with a pop. "Turn around and grip the counter."

Oh, God. It's exactly like my fantasy. I swear he has inside access into my head.

I do as I'm told. My blood is rushing through me, igniting every nerve. He rubs a palm over my ass cheek, squeezing hard, almost painfully.

"One day when you've sassed me, you're going to wear my handprint right here."

I wiggle my hips, pushing my ass out, daring him. I throb when I hear the zipper on his slacks drop. I want to look at his cock, see it—hold it—taste it.

"I'm going to take you roughly this first time, Sof, because I can't fucking restrain myself. Hold on tight, okay?"

"Okay," I whimper, so desperate to feel him inside me.

Kicking my feet with his still shoe-covered foot, he parts my legs for me and then he's there, prodding at me. His thick head pushes against my opening, and I almost sag in relief when he thrusts forward, filling me up. The entry robs me of breath and stings, but the pain and pleasure send me rocketing to the fucking moon. I can't get enough. He thunders into me, and I push back to meet him thrust for thrust. His outstretched palms grip my hips to give him extra momentum. My arousal drips over his cock and then down my thighs. I've never been this turned on in my entire life or ever reached this kind of release on my own. Quakes tremble through me as pleasure rolls over me in shock waves. I use the counter for support, laying my top half down on the cold granite as he thrusts and grunts.

"I'm going to come." He sounds feral and hungry.

"Fill me up, Daddy," I moan, squeezing my walls around him.

"Fuck, fuck, fuck," he groans, as warm cum ripples from him, flooding my womb.

Oh, crap.

I'm on the pill, but letting some guy I barely know come inside me is as reckless as it gets. So why do I still feel safe? Like he'd never expose me to anything dangerous. And if I were to get pregnant, he'd take care of me. He's inside my mind, taking root, and I like it.

I like it so much it scares me.

"I want to hear your voice crying out all night for me," he murmurs, slipping out of me and helping me stand. He spins me around to face him and then lifts me. I wrap my legs around his waist and curl against his muscular chest.

"I'm going to keep you up for days, Sof," he vows in a playful tone, squeezing my ass. "I hope you have stamina."

"I've got more than you, old man," I tease. He's not old. Not by a long shot. But it feels exciting to tease and test him. "I can handle it."

His features darken, not disappointing me one bit.

"Hmmm," he grinds out, playfully swatting my ass. "I'll have to punish you for that."

9

Ronan

Leave her alone, Ronan.

You wore the poor little girl out last night.

A grin tugs at my lips as I run my finger along her arm as she sleeps. Her plump lips are parted and her dark lashes fan across her apple cheeks. I need to get up and shower to go into the office, but I can't fucking take my eyes off her.

Bruises made from my mouth color her creamy neck, filling me with male, possessive pride. She'll have a helluva time covering that shit up. Everyone will know she's been claimed.

Her eyes flutter open and when she sees me, she smiles. "Morning." The sexy rasp of her voice makes my dick really fucking hard.

"Morning, sweetheart."

She tentatively strokes her fingers down my hard abs toward my dick that's been eager all morning, but I stop her with my words.

"Don't start something you can't finish," I warn.

Her hand stills and she cocks a brow. "I was planning on finishing."

"I fucked you raw last night, Sof. Trust me, you need to let your pretty little pussy rest."

"Maybe I like it raw," she sasses.

"You don't know what you like." I challenge her with a lifted brow. "Trust me to look after you."

Her blue eyes flare. "I can look after myself."

"Keep it up…"

She presses her lips together. "Keep it up…or what?"

I know she likes being a good little girl, but sometimes good girls like to be bad.

"Or I'll take my belt to your ass," I say in a deep, throaty growl. "Redden it up and make you cry. Teach you what happens when you sass me about your well-being. I've been around long enough to know what a girl like you needs and when she needs it."

"Maybe I'm different," she argues, continuing to run that beautiful mouth of hers.

"Fuck yes, you're different, but the rules still apply."

Ignoring me, she sits up and slides her leg over my lap to straddle me. "See? I'm fine."

Reaching between us, I push a finger into her. The stubborn girl winces but refuses to acknowledge the fact she's been overly fucked and needs a damn rest. I pull my finger out and show her.

"See how dry this finger is?"

"I don't care," she says, pouting. "I can handle a little pain."

Gripping her hips, I toss her aside and climb out of the bed. Her blue eyes flash with panic, as though she's actually pissed me off. No, her defying me turns me the fuck on.

"A little pain, hmmm?" I taunt as I walk over to my discarded slacks. Bending over, I pull my belt from the hoops. "Good, because you've earned this pain fair and square."

I sit on the edge of the bed and fold the belt in half. With a playful swat, I hit her thigh over the covers. "Lie across my lap, little badass."

"You're really going to whip me?" she asks, her voice slightly trembling with horror and shock.

"I really am, Sof. You asked for it. Practically

begged for it. It's okay to be a bad girl sometimes too. My dick certainly seems to think so."

She slowly crawls toward me. "Will I cry?"

My grin is wolfish. "You might."

"Then what?"

"Then I'll make it all better."

She tentatively slides her body across my thighs. Tiny little thing weighs nothing. Her tits hang down and her round ass is ripe for the taking. My dick is sandwiched between her ribs and my stomach. Each time she wriggles against it, I suppress a groan.

"Stay still," I command, swatting her ass softly.

Her body freezes.

"You really are a good girl," I murmur. "How many swats do you think you deserve since it's your first time for misbehaving?"

She wiggles again. "I don't know. One?"

A laugh rumbles from me. "One? You know better than that, sweetheart. How about one swat for every time I fucked your sore little pussy last night."

"Four," she breathes.

"Four," I agree. "I must warn you, I have a heavy hand."

"What if I can't take it?"

"You can because you're strong," I tell her fiercely. "But in the event you can't, we can have a safe word. My ultimate goal is to take care of you. It's why you're getting punished in the first place. Because you wouldn't let me take care of you." I run the leather down between her thighs toward her knees and then back up again toward her ass crack. "Go on, let me know the safe word."

"Ummm, stop?"

I chuckle. "You can do better than that."

"Kinky bastard?"

"That's two, but I like it." I stroke my finger down her spine. "Ready?"

"Yes," she breathes.

Rather than whipping her with the folded belt, I straighten it and fist the buckle. Then, I wrap the length around my fist to shorten it and clutch onto another section of the belt. It leaves a nice foot's worth of length to use. Her right cheek will bear the brunt of this whipping because of our position. I'll switch it up next time.

There's always a next time.

Without any more warning, I strike down on her ass cheek. She screams out in horror, her body straightening at the pain of it.

"Ow! Ronan! That hurt!" I can hear the emotion in her voice. A slight tremble. The shock of me actually carrying through with the punishment.

Whap!

This time when I strike her cheek beside the last red stripe mark, she makes a choked sound and tries to climb off me. I grip her hip and squeeze it.

"You have a safe word. Use it, Sof, if you need it. But if you don't need it, then I suggest you keep your ass right here and take the punishment you earned."

"You hit me harder than I expected." She pouts.

"Was I supposed to go easy on you?" I challenge. "If I went easy, it wouldn't make me a good, firm daddy, now would it?"

Whap!

A sob escapes her. Her ass cheek is bright red from her whippings. I pause, ready to give her the out she needs. When she doesn't say her safe word, I strike her one last time, hard. Her entire body quakes as she breaks down in tears. I toss the belt and twist her around to where she's sitting in my lap. She winces at the pain of her ass against my thigh. Hugging her to me, I kiss the top of her head and stroke her hair.

"I really am a kinky bastard," I tell her, my voice soft. "I'm not sure how I came to be this way."

Her crying softens as she listens, seemingly eager to know more about me.

"You know, my mom died when I was a young man, and I had to raise my brother Ren. I was no longer a big brother, but his caretaker. Much like a father. And now I'm technically his boss. It's ingrained in me to want to control things for the ones I care about. I only have their best interest at heart."

"And me?" she whimpers. "You care about me?"

"From the moment I saw you."

"Why?"

"Something about your personality called to mine. You want to be taken care of. Not like how your brother does it, but for someone to really care for you with no strings attached." I kiss her head again. "It makes me happy to make you happy. It's as simple as that. The kink part of it in the bedroom is hot as fuck, but this is a lifestyle for me. Something that goes beyond the bedroom and is engrained in who I am. If the spanking was too much or you're not sure you like it, tell me upfront, sweetheart. Don't let our hearts get tangled first and then leave me hanging later."

"It hurt." The pout in her voice does nothing to help the state of my cock. In fact, it twitches against her.

"It was meant to. All lessons hurt in some way."

"I really wanted you to make love to me again,"

she whispers. "I didn't expect to be so sore from having sex."

I chuckle, squeezing her to me. "It's not your fault I last so damn long. When you're my age, you learn to control when you come and can draw that need out longer. It's also not your fault that my cock's so big."

She laughs but doesn't argue. "So you still want me? You just didn't want to hurt me?"

"Of course I fucking want you," I rumble. "And if you had been a good girl, I would have told you we had other ways to play—ways to please us both. But you were stubborn and wanted your way. It doesn't work like that in this relationship."

"So you get to boss me around?" The sass is back in her voice.

"I get to take care of you. You will allow me to because it gets me off and makes me happy. I like taking care of you. Being cared for gets you off and makes you happy. We're two parts of a whole…a little incomplete on our own."

She turns her head up to look at me. "You've done this before, though. The whole daddy thing. Am I just another…" Her nose scrunches as she bites on her bottom lip, worry shimmering in her blue eyes.

"Another what?"

"Another little girl with daddy issues? Someone for you to fix?"

I roll my eyes at her. "I don't fix people and move on. I am like any other human being out there—searching for someone to fill voids within me. When I saw you, certain holes that always remain unfilled were brimming with light. I fucking needed you like I needed air. Understand, sweetheart? You're different and I knew it even before you opened your mouth and sang like an angel." I kiss her pouty mouth. "I'd be stupid not to pounce on something so perfect. Maybe that makes me greedy and selfish. I call it seeing what you want and fucking taking it."

Her lips curl into a smile. "So I'm not a fling? Because I totally screwed things up with my brother to take this chance with you."

I brush her hair from her face. "Your brother will come back around. If he's anything like my brother, he'll be pissed for a bit but then come crawling back with his tail between his legs. You two will patch shit up. In the meantime, you'll stay with me."

She widens her innocent, blue eyes. "Like live here?"

"Yes," I growl, my dick achingly hard at the prospect of having her in my bed every night.

"That's fast, isn't it?"

"Is there an instruction manual on these things I missed reading? A time limit set by the government? Did someone tell you that you must date someone a certain amount of time before it's allowable to move in with him?"

She snorts. "Who's the sassy one now?

"I think we call it being an arrogant prick, but sassy is cute." I waggle my brows at her. "I'm not always stern and making rules. I can have fun too."

A brilliant smile spreads across her face. "I've had more fun in the past few days since I met you than I've had in my entire life."

"To be fair," I tease, "your life was kind of boring to begin with."

"Hey now," she grumbles, still grinning.

"I have to go into the office later, but first, I want to do to you what I planned on doing before you started trying to run this show." I smirk at her. "Who's in control here, sweetheart?"

"You," she says breathily.

"And who am I?"

Her cheeks burn pink. "Daddy."

"Lie back on the pillows while I get what I need," I instruct.

She crawls away onto the bed, seemingly eager

to escape my intense stare. Once she's settled, I walk over to the end table and pull out the lube. Then, I make my way across the bed on my knees and then sit on my haunches. I settle between her legs and spread them. Her cunt is bright red and slightly swollen like I knew it would be. Setting the lube down, I grip her hips and drag her up my thighs so her pelvis is tilted up toward me.

"What are you doing?" she breathes.

"I'm going to get you feeling much better and soon."

I open the cap on the lube and squirt out a heap of it on her lower stomach. She hisses at the coldness of it. After I close the bottle and toss it, I flatten out my hands and rub my palms through the lube. Her breath hitches when I slide my palms up along her ribcage and then massage her gorgeous tits. I take the time to lube up her nipples with my thumbs until they're hard, dark pink nubs. Then, I slide my palms down her flat stomach to right above her pussy. Her hips tilt up, seeking my touch there, but I purposefully ignore that place. Instead, I slide my lubed hands along the apex of her thighs and then down her upper legs to her knees. She whines when I run them over her hips and then around to her backside. I grip her right cheek extra hard, making her wince, before sliding back around to the front.

"Ronan," she whimpers. "Please."

I smirk as I tease my thumbs along her red pussy lips, gently, and then I'm back to massaging her thighs. Her tits jiggle more frantically with each eager breath she takes.

"Your nipples need attention, Sof. I want to see you pulling at them."

She bites on her lip, a shy flush creeping up her neck. But she obeys because she's fucking perfect. Her thumb and finger of each hand pinch each nipple as she tugs. To reward her, I brush my thumb over her clit. Briefly. A moan escapes her.

"Harder, sweetheart. I want to see how hard you can pull them."

Her blue eyes darken with lust as she pulls them up.

"Don't let go," I instruct. "Pull as hard as you can until you think you can't take it anymore."

She winces in pain but does as she's told. When her helpless blue eyes lock with mine, I grin wickedly at her.

"Now twist them."

Panic flashes in her eyes, but then her wrists swivel with the motion. Her back arches up off the bed. I find her clit with my thumb and rub firm circles on it.

"Can I let go?" she whines.

"No," I growl. "I want you to keep it up until I tell you to stop."

Another whimper.

My pointer finger joins my thumb and I roll her clit between the two digits, not unlike how she's twisting her own nipples. I tug hard twice in a row, before rolling the throbbing nub again. I repeat this action until she's writhing uncontrollably with need.

"Please," she begs. "It hurts."

I chuckle, not giving in, and push her thigh up toward her to open her cunt to me. It glistens with her arousal. While I pinch and pull at her clit, I use my knuckles on my other hand to tease along her slit that slightly parts for me. It's red and sore looking, so I'm gentle with her. I never enter her pussy, simply make her body beg for it.

"You can take a break," I tell her.

She releases her tits and breathes heavily, awaiting my next instruction.

"Do your clit now," I command. "Like I taught you."

Her brows furrow together, but she snakes her hand down her stomach. She tenderly touches the nub and begins mimicking my actions. I pick up the lube and uncap it. Our eyes meet when I pour a healthy amount on her pussy and let some run down her crack. She uses the lubricant to rub at her clit, her fingers moving quickly and eagerly.

I smack at her hand. "I didn't say get yourself off, sweetheart. I said to pinch your clit. Pull on it. Make it hurt."

She glowers at me. Sassy fucking girl. At least she obeys. When she goes back to torturing herself, I rub the lube all over her cunt and even ease my thumb inside of her. The dirty girl clenches around it and lifts her hips as to fuck it, but I pull it out before she can find too much pleasure in it.

"Straddle my thighs and get back to work," I growl, smacking her cunt again.

Her eyes flare with lust and she sits up quickly. Once her legs are spread on my thighs and my throbbing dick is bouncing eagerly between us, she slides her fingers back down to abuse her clit. I rub her sore ass, spreading the lube all over her ass cheeks. She flinches when my finger slides along her crack.

"How do you feel about anal?"

Her body trembles. "I've never done it."

"Do you want to one day?"

"Y-Yes, I think."

"It'll take some prep work, but we can try it," I murmur, kissing her shoulder as I tease her asshole with my finger. "I love anal, sweetheart. And would give anything to put my cock inside you there one day."

"I want you to," she murmurs.

"You know the safe word."

Slowly, I push into the tight ring of her ass, inching my finger inside of her. She whimpers, tightening around me. With my free hand, I slap her sore ass cheek hard.

"Relax," I bark out, nipping at her shoulder.

"Ohhh," she whines.

"Keep pinching that clit, sweetheart. If you want to get nice and juicy to ride my dick, you need to obey me."

"Okay, Ronan."

"No," I growl. "You can do better than that."

"Daddy," she breathes. "Yes, Daddy."

I smile against her shoulder and kiss the flesh. "Good, good girl, Sofina."

She lets out a sharp cry when I start fucking her ass with my finger. "It burns."

"It's supposed to," I tell her. "That's what makes it feel so forbidden and taboo. Like I'm not supposed to be there."

Another whimper.

"But I'm there, aren't I? I don't care what the rules are, I'm there and you'll learn to like it, won't you?"

"Y-Yes, Daddy."

"I'm going to slide another finger in there to stretch you out a bit. It's okay to cry, beautiful. Remember your safe word and I'll take my fingers out." I lick her salty skin. "It's okay to get yourself off now. Rub it until you come and then keep rubbing, baby. I want you to come as many times as you can."

Her hand massages between us as she does as she's told. While she's distracted, I ease another finger into her ass. She's tight as fuck here and one day I'll go fucking crazy being able to slide in and out of it until I fill her up.

"Ow," she whimpers.

"Ow isn't a safe word," I remind her.

I grip her sore ass cheek, spreading her open more to accommodate both fingers. I press them inside as far as they'll go, rotating them in a semicircle to stretch her tiny hole.

"Oh, God!" she cries out, shuddering. Her hand flies to my shoulder as she clutches onto me tightly enough to break the skin. I continue to fuck her ass with my two fingers as she rides her orgasm right into another one. When her fingers stop moving, I growl.

"Don't stop, Sof."

"I can't do it anymore," she whimpers tearfully. "I'm exhausted."

"One more time and I'll let you jack me off all over your tight stomach."

My determined girl goes back to rubbing on her overstimulated clit. Her breathing is heavy and raspy. When she wrings out another orgasm, I can't help but grin in pride. Immediately, her hand wraps around my dick, eager to please. I can barely keep up with the pace of fingering her ass as she strokes me.

Knowing she's weakening by the second, I give in to the urge to come. My muscles tighten in anticipation. With a groan, I shoot my load between us, making a big fucking mess.

"Lie back now," I instruct, my voice husky with lingering pleasure. "Easy now. I want to show you something."

Clumsily, she falls back onto the bed, her legs still wide-open with my two fingers in her ass.

"Hold your legs behind your knees and spread yourself apart. I want you to look at what I'm doing to you." Our eyes meet and her face blazes crimson. "Now, Sofina."

She pulls back her thighs and then curls up to watch where I have my fingers in her ass.

"I like seeing you stretched out around me," I tell her, smiling. "One day, when I slide my dick inside you here, I want you to film it."

"You want me to make an anal sex tape?"

I laugh. "We can watch it together later."

"You're filthy," she accuses, her blue eyes flickering with lust.

"Says the girl with two fingers in her ass."

Using my other hand, I collect my cum from my stomach and then slide two fingers into her cunt. She gasps at the fullness of being filled in two holes. I fuck her ass and pussy with my fingers gently. Curling my two fingers up, I seek out her G-spot that seems swollen and eager for attention. The moment I touch it, she whines.

"Ronan…"

"Make yourself come again, Sof. I gave you time to rest. Now it's time to work."

She shakes her head. "I c-can't."

"Try for me, baby."

Determination once again fuels my good girl. Her fingers rub at her clit. Each time she touches it, her body trembles. She rubs it at first, but when she doesn't get the result she's after, she takes to rolling it between her fingers again and then tugging on it. Seems as though she enjoys the pain a little. Her tits jiggle as she desperately tries to come. I simply tease her G-spot, but never really give her the orgasm she seeks. Her body breaks out in a sheen of sweat and her brows furl together in fierce concentration. I rub her more firmly from within, with more purpose to drive her closer to the edge.

"Daddy," she whimpers. "I want to come."

"Then come, Sof."

She starts rubbing her clit in fast circles, her flesh making a slapping sound. I fuck her with my fingers more quickly to match her movement, really putting pressure on her G-spot. The moment I can tell she's about to fall over the cliff, I rub inside her hard and fast. My sweet, perfect girl doesn't disappoint. A gush of heat rushes out, forcing my fingers back. I fuck her cunt probably too hard with my fingers, but she's squirting and I want her to ride this literal wave, with every nerve ending on fire. She screams—her voice sounding otherworldly and pained—as her body thrashes. The liquid pleasure bursting from her slows to a trickle. Slowly, I slide both hands from her body.

"You made a mess," I tease, admiring the juices from her body that have splattered my thighs, stomach, and hands.

Her face burns red. "I'm sorry."

"Sorry for being fucking perfect? Sorry for letting me play your body as it was meant to be played? Sorry for helping me get you to a level of ecstasy that is hardly achieved?"

"Well," she sasses, her tits still jiggling as she fights to catch her breath, "when you put it that way, I'm not sorry."

I playfully swat her sore, wet pussy. "Good girl. Now let's get you in the shower. I have to go to work. Now that your cunt is juiced up and ready for me, I won't be able to leave until I've fucked you. And I don't want to be late for work. My new superstar is meeting with her talent manager and I need to see to it she's well taken care of."

10

Sofina

Three weeks later…

Bastian slaps his notepad and grins at me. "Yes. This is exactly what I was thinking when I thought up these lyrics."

I grip the mic and growl out the last few words, throwing every bit of passion into them. When I finish, he stands and claps his hands.

"Bravo, little star. I knew these lyrics wouldn't be wasted on you." He gives me a four-fingered wave. "I'm going to run to the ladies' room and when I get back, we'll take it from the top."

As he bounces off, I can't help but giggle. Bastian is the crookedest straight man I've ever met. He wears leather pants more often than not, has bleached blond hair that looks nearly purple in the light, and wears glitter on his lips. I'd think the most sought after songwriter on the East Coast was gay, but he's married to a brunette actress and has three adorable kids.

My smile falls when I check my phone. No calls or messages from Lucca. It's been three weeks I've spent with Ronan that I haven't spoken to my brother. I never officially quit, but through texts with Ruby and Hollie, I learned that he hired another bartender in my absence.

Everything would be perfect if things weren't so broken with Lucca.

I consider texting him, but what would I say? I hope you're having fun being your usual miserable self while my daddy spoils me with continuous orgasms, fancy dinners, and lavish gifts…oh, and all the while getting to do my dream job. No, I certainly won't say that, even if it is the truth. Deep down, I know my brother wants me to be happy. I wish he'd find ways to make himself happy, too.

"Sweetie pie," Bastian calls out, dragging me from my thoughts. "The wifey called and Gigi is throwing up. Apparently my new white rug is wearing the proof." He groans. "Leslie can't do puke, which means I must go save the day."

I walk over to him and give him a hug. "I'll keep working on this track. I think it could be the single."

"And keep working on yours too," he encourages, his green eyes glimmering softly. "You're not only a talented voice, you've got a brain for writing lyrics too. 'Take Care of Me' could be a hit, Sofina."

Blushing at his praise, I wave him off. "Oh, stop."

"I'll do nothing of the sort," he playfully huffs. "Now, toodaloo. I'll see you tomorrow."

Once he's gone, I close up the sound room and lock the door before heading upstairs to the executive offices. Ren's office is nearly empty all the time, but I like when I get to chat with him. He's super talented and has great ideas. But my favorite guy to talk to is the head man in charge. Our talks always lead to naughty things, but I'm not complaining.

I make my way down the hallway to his closed door. He's talking to one of his clients from the sound of it and both men are arguing heatedly. Eve, his prissy secretary, is on the phone with someone, so I loiter awkwardly. I'd leave except Ronan specifically asked me to come see him after my session with Bastian.

"I know, Starla," Eve placates. "And he did take care of you, but that's over now and you can't call every time you see something you want. Your time together has ended."

I stiffen and pay attention to her conversation. "He already has a new girl. You knew this is what he was like when you chose to be with him."

Starla replies, but I don't know what she's saying.

"She's talented, yes." A pause. "Well, I think it may be serious. It'd do you some good to move on. That was the agreement. Aren't you enjoying the new car?"

The new car.

I get a gross, icky feeling. It's not like he wasn't upfront about being a daddy, but hearing about the others he took care of makes my stomach roil.

"I'll tell him you called, but he won't return your phone call no matter how much you try to provoke him. Have you tried online dating? That's how I met Gary. Maybe you can find a sugar daddy to buy you nice things."

I've met her husband, Gary. Tall, nerdy guy who loves her and their thirteen-month-old son Carson. I'm happy for her finding Gary, but totally skeeved out that Starla is calling her pining for Ronan.

He's mine.

At least I thought.

Right now, it feels like maybe he's mine only for right now.

Until when?

"Okay, Starla, I need to go. I have appointments to keep. Turns out one of Ren's new finds used to be a stripper. It's going to be a PR nightmare, so we have her coming in for a meeting with Ronan." A chuckle. "Of course she has tits, she was a stripper." Another pause. "Okay. It was nice to hear from you, but I think it's best if you distance yourself from this place now and focus on your degree. Bye now."

She hangs up the phone and, as if sensing me, turns. Her eyes widen. "Sofina, darling, I didn't see you standing there. Something I can help you with?"

Yeah, I need a freaking cracker and a ginger ale because I think I'm going to be sick.

"Here to see Mr. Hayes," I mumble.

She purses her lips together. "He's meeting with one of his bands. They should be done any—"

"What the fuck ever, Hayes," a man bellows, stumbling slightly as he charges out of Ronan's office. "All you ever care about is the bottom line. I fucking hate you and this label."

Ronan storms after him, his face red with fury. "Xavi, this label pays your goddamn bills, you ungrateful piece of shit. How about you sober the fuck up and we'll talk about renegotiating your contract. Until then, stay the hell away from here."

Xavi flips him off and kicks over a plant on the

way out. When Ronan's furious glare meets mine, he visibly softens.

"Hey, sweetheart. Come here."

I shakily make my way over to him. Once I'm in his warm, strong arms and inhaling his familiar, masculine scent, I can't help but want to forget the yucky stuff I overheard Eve and Starla saying. Almost.

"What's wrong?" he demands, already knowing me all too well.

"Nothing," I croak.

"Not nothing," he grumbles. "You're shaking. Are you sick?" Then, to Eve, he barks out, "Cancel my afternoon appointment. Have Brennan meet with her. I'll look over the proposal before we offer her anything."

As soon as Eve busies herself calling Brennan, Ronan tugs me into his office and closes the door behind him.

"I can tell when you're lying, Sof," he says in a soft tone. "Something's wrong. What is it?"

Tears flood my eyes. "Everything and nothing," I choke out pitifully. "I have a dream job and a dream boyfriend. My life is perfect."

"But…" he urges.

"But my brother hates me."

"He doesn't hate you. And this isn't new. What else is it?"

With a huff, I step back and cross my arms over my chest. "I understand you have a past with other little girls like me, but I don't like having it flaunted in my face."

His brows lift. "Elaborate."

My bottom lip wobbles. "Eve and Starla. I overheard Eve talking to your ex-girlfriend." And while he'd been upfront about his most recent relationship, I didn't think about the girls who came before me until today. "Starla still wants you."

He presses his lips into a firm line and narrows his eyes. "I only want you, Sof. I'm pretty sure I've made this abundantly clear." He steps closer, and I wilt at his alluring nearness. "I didn't move any girl besides you into my home."

"You bought them cars instead," I state bitterly.

He lets out a heavy sigh. "Look, I won't apologize for the man I am. All my past relationships have led me to this place. But while they were simply tests or experimental relationships, no one but you has ever gripped me by the heart and demanded my undivided attention. All I see is you, Sof."

When he pulls me into a hug, I soften and rest my cheek on his chest.

"I wrote a song," I breathe. "I wanted to surprise you with it. I just…it has to do with you taking care of me, and now…"

"Now what?"

"It feels cheapened." The truth hurts.

He grips my jaw and tilts my head up. His intense brown eyes sear into mine. "Nothing about what we do—what we are is cheap. Don't let a few words of others work their way into your head and make you doubt us. The moment I saw you, I dropped Starla. She was for passing time until I found the right one."

"And I'm the right one?" I ask. "Until the stripper shows up?"

His features harden. "I've allowed your tantrum, sweetheart, but now you're getting disrespectful and I've done nothing to deserve it."

The disappointment in his features has me bursting into tears. Normally, him spanking me turns me on, but right now, I feel like I've let him down by letting self-doubt get me down. He hugs me tight and kisses the top of my head.

"Listen to me, sweetheart. I love us. I love being with you. I love hearing you sing in the mornings when you get dressed for the day. I love watching you sleep and the way you cry out when you lose yourself to an orgasm. I love shopping and dining with you. I love being with you." He places his palms on my cheeks and kisses my forehead. "Take away all the kink of what we are, and I still love us. Got it?"

"I'm sorry," I say sadly.

"Don't be sorry," he croons. "I'd be pissed as fuck if I had to hear about your ex-boyfriends talking about how much they still want you. I get it and I'll have a talk with Eve to keep her personal conversations to her lunch hour. But promise me you'll squash my past and live in the present with me."

I smile at him. "I promise."

"And I can't wait to hear that song, Sof. You're so fucking talented." He beams at me. "Bastian says you're a natural with songwriting. I had no doubts, which is why I wanted you having ultimate creative control with your music." He playfully pinches my cheek. "I was taking care of my little girl long before she knew it."

God, he's so sexy when he's playful.

I slide my palm down to the front of his slacks and rub him until his cock is straining against the fabric.

"Now you're being a bad girl," he growls. "You

know I like to keep the work stuff separate from the hot as hell stuff. The banter and flirting and hugging and kissing is fine, but—"

I pull at his buckle. "Did you fuck them in here?"

His eyes darken. "No. I told—"

"Did they suck you off in here?" I interrupt, unfastening his pants and pulling his dick into my hand.

"No."

"Good," I purr as I drop to my knees. "This makes me different, right?"

He groans and his eyes roll back when I lick his crown. "Fuck, yes, sweetheart."

I take him fully in my mouth, loving the painful grip on my hair as he loses control to the pleasure.

"Jesus, Sof, you're going to kill me."

Sliding off his dick, I look up at him and grin. "I'm marking my territory and staking my claim."

His eyes flash with darkness and lust. "You're still getting punished for breaking the rules."

I tease the slit on the tip of his dick with my tongue, giving him my best innocent eyes. "You'll probably have to bend me over your desk and spank me."

He growls in warning, his grip on my hair tightening.

"And so your clients and ex-girlfriends don't hear us, you better get creative in keeping me quiet."

His hips thrust hard, effectively shutting my sassy mouth up.

11

Ronan

Gazing at Sofina's curves outlined by a beautiful black dress makes me want to rethink bringing her with me to meet Ren at a bar where one of our artists is playing tonight. All eyes stray to her as she passes and pride blossoms in my chest. She's mine. They can look, but she leaves with me. *Is it time to go yet?*

"I love it here, Ronan. The ambiance of this bar is everything I wanted for Ritz Russo's. Every table occupied with groups of people drinking and having fun and the stage the focal point of the club." She beams at me, a gracious smile on her luscious lips. "Lucca always shot my ideas down."

Placing my hand on her lower back, I guide her

to a corner booth sectioned off for us. Ren is already sitting there nursing a beer. This place is one of the most popular clubs in town and influential in the music industry. Many talents have launched from this very club. The wait list to get into their open mic night is six months long.

Sofina leans over to drop a kiss to Ren's cheek, making him grin up at me like a fool. The asshole. I slide into the booth beside her and flag down a waitress.

"One lemon drop and a whiskey on the rocks," I instruct. "Bring the bottle and an extra glass, please."

"That extra glass better not be for me," my brother complains like the pussy bitch he is now that he has a girlfriend. "I have plans after this. I can't be comatose on hundred-dollar whiskey by nine o'clock."

"Since when did you not want to be drunk by nine o clock? Oh, wait, since you handed your balls over to a certain lady," I mock, making Sofina giggle.

"I love this place, Ren. How did you find it? There's a relaxed vibe, but there's no mistake you're in an expensive place being treated to something exceptional, you know? I wish Lucca would come to places like this and see what's out there, what works." She rants on, making Ren raise a questioning brow in my direction.

"What's the deal with your brother anyway?" Ren asks blatantly.

Her little body sags slightly. Lucca has fucking issues. Sofina thinks he's ignoring her and letting her go, but the truth is he's been calling me at work, grieving to me about her.

He wants her home. Chucked the word brat around until I hung up on him five times.

Something is going to have to be done. He may be a fucking prick, but she loves him and misses him.

"He gave up a lot. Came home to take care of me so I didn't get put into the foster system," Sofina says, with a shrug of her shoulder. Our drinks arrive, offering her a reprieve from Ren interrogating her.

"What did he give up?" Ren asks once the waitress leaves.

"Ren," I bark, shaking my head.

A light chuckle tickles from Sofina as she places a hand on my arm. "It's fine." She takes a sip of her drink and stirs it with her finger before slipping the digit into her mouth and sucking the juice from it.

For fuck's sake.

It's innocent on her part, but she has no clue how sexual she is by a simple action. Ren's eyes flick to her finger, then lips, and then over to me with a filthy smirk tilting up his mouth.

Fucker. He's thinking the exact thing I am.

"School, but it was a girl who broke him, you know?" she muses, her brow crashing down.

"She dumped him?" Ren asks, making me roll my eyes. This shit isn't our business.

"He asked her to move back with him, but she wouldn't. It really took a toll on him."

Ren keeps on fucking probing. "Do you feel blame?"

"Ren," I growl. He smiles and leans in on his forearms to get a better look at Sofina, daring her to answer.

"Yes, but I was a kid and didn't ask him to make that choice."

"He's your brother. It was never a choice," I tell her, stroking a finger down her cheek.

"Family is everything. Your brother will come around. Don't fret, little pet," Ren says, pouring a whiskey into the spare glass and replacing her lemon drop with it.

I feel it as her spine straightens. Her head turns

to me with her eyes expanding. "I don't like liquor." She scrunches up her nose. It's adorable, and it turns me on more than I could ever explain to her.

"You'll like this. Go ahead, sweetheart, numb the chaos and sample a real whiskey." I wink at her.

She wraps her nimble fingers around the glass and gulps the amber liquid like it's a fucking soda. Her eyes widen impossibly big, and then she coughs and waves a hand over her tongue, making both Ren and me burst into a bout of laughter.

She grabs the lemon drop from Ren and gulps it down. "Oh my God, it burns. I hate whiskey," she whines.

Ren slaps the table and holds his hand up to the waitress. "Bring ice and lemon drops. Keep them coming." Then he turns to Sofina, laughing. "Don't you own a bar?"

"Our whiskey is watered down and I don't drink the stock."

"Wussy," he teases.

A round of applause sounds through the room as a guy takes to the mic to introduce the next act. "Please give a warm embrace for Nina Rose."

"This is our artist. The one I was supposed to meet with," I whisper against Sofina's earlobe and groan when she leans into me and shivers.

Nina's guitar strums and a few whistles pierce the air before an alluring pulse croons from her lips, filtering into the mic and floating over the audience. She has a country style about her and highly sellable. Everyone in the audience, including the three of us, are captured by her music.

When she finishes up, Sofina mumbles, "Her tits aren't even that big."

Ren chokes on his drink, spitting half of it down himself. "Why does that matter?"

I watch a crimson glow redden her cheeks when she realizes she spoke aloud. "Oh, sorry, Eve said she was a stripper and had big boobs."

Ren's phone buzzes with an incoming text that has him grinning and licking his lips.

"Care to share?" I tease him, getting him back for eyeballing Sofina's sucking skills earlier.

"Not in this lifetime." He flicks beer from the table in my direction before flitting his thumbs over the phone with a reply. "She's not a typical stripper," Ren pipes up before slipping his phone away into his pocket.

"What does that mean?" I drum my fingers on the table and with the other arm drag Sofina onto my lap so I can feel her ass against my cock.

"I mean, she's a high paid dancer. She's behind a

screen in a members-only club. Not out on a pole at a biker dive."

"Still a PR nightmare if it gets out," I groan.

"Artists pole dance in music videos these days, Ronan," Ren argues.

"That's true and look at those lady rappers. They sing about their snatches all the time," Sofina says, shuddering. And again, Ren and I burst into a fit of laughter.

When we settle down, Ren nods back to the stage and asks, "She's good, right?"

"I like her," Sofina announces with a sigh. "I'd love to be able to sing in a place like this with her confidence and talent."

"You have more talent," I remind her. "And if you want to sing here you can."

"You want me to go speak to the manager? He's a friend." Ren winks at her, and she looks up at me expectantly.

Without waiting for a reply, Ren scoots out of the booth and waltzes off.

"He's joking, right?" she breathes.

"Nope." I grin, nibbling her neck.

"Oh, God. I'll be too nervous," she whispers.

"Let me help relax you then," I rumble, slipping my hand up her dress to brush over her lace-covered pussy. "Be a good girl and part these legs, sweetheart."

She does as she's told, allowing me access to slip beneath her panties and insert a finger into her cunt.

Wet and needy as always.

Delicious.

Her breathing becomes ragged as I tease and taunt her with the promise of an orgasm. Her hand grips my wrist and guides my movements. I allow her to take control, knowing I'll be dominating her ass later.

She groans and it makes my dick harden. She squirms and rotates her hips. I nip her lip and use my thumb to circle her clit. Her pussy walls clamp and pulse. Her breathing hitches. I kiss her cries away as she comes over my fingers.

"Better?" I lick her lips.

"Yes, so much."

When Ren returns, he's not alone. Nina stands with him nervously picking at her fingers.

"Nina, you were amazing. I'm Sofina," my girl says to put her at ease, offering her a hand to shake.

"Thank you." Nina smiles and glances over at me briefly before looking away.

"Sofina, you're on in an hour," Ren informs her. "I can't stick around, but I know you'll do great.

Nina's going to take you backstage so you can practice and get ready. Brother, I'll call you." With that, he pats Nina on the back and takes off.

Sofina waits for me to say something, her ass not moving from my lap. I hold in a chuckle, tapping her ass to encourage her to go. "You're going to be amazing. And you're in good hands. Good job tonight, Nina. You're going to have a fruitful career."

"Thank you, sir." Nina beams at us.

·····◆·····

My hand tightens around my glass when I see Lucca walking toward me, a scowl on his face. Prick. I called him once Sofina scampered away and told him to meet me here before hanging up. I didn't know if he would show, but I needed to know I tried for my girl.

He slips into the booth and glares over at me, arms resting on the table. He's out of place here with his tattoos and attitude. "Got in okay then?" I smirk. I had his name added to the guest list, and I know it pisses him off that I can pull strings he can't.

The thing he needs to learn is this isn't a pissing contest. I'd win, and it's pointless. We both want the same thing, I hope—Sofina's happiness.

"What the hell do you want, Hayes?" he growls.

I pour a drink and shove it across the table toward him. "Drink."

He picks up the glass, swirls the amber liquid, and then sniffs it before taking a swig. Like he has any clue about the quality of the whiskey.

"This why you brought me here? To show me you can afford the good whiskey?" he sneers.

"That good whiskey is what you should be pouring at your place. It has the potential to be a great bar. It's in a great location."

He holds a hand up and shakes his head to stop my talking. "What is this? You want to talk about my bar?"

"No, I want to talk about your sister."

"Where the fuck is my sister?" he growls, leaning toward me. The friction is palpable in the air between us.

"She's going to be performing, and I wanted you to see her."

Snorting, he grabs the bottle of whiskey and pours himself another, leaving my glass empty. He reminds me of when Ren went through a rebellious phase. Hated the world for the shitty cards it dealt our mother.

"I've seen her sing. She's been singing since before she could talk."

"Then why do you not want her to pursue her dream?"

Grinding his jaw, he narrows his eyes on me before sighing and knocking back the drink. "I didn't want it to eat her up and chew her out. I didn't want her dreams tarnished by disappointment and opportunists." He glares at me like I'm some predator.

"So you wanted to keep her as Cinderella in your dive bar?"

"Fuck you, man. I only keep that place so she has something. A place to provide for her," he says with a heavy sigh, rubbing his hands down his face. "I fucking hate that place and I failed her anyway."

"What does that mean?" Color me curious.

Folding his arms, he stares off into the crowd for a few silent beats. "The bar's a money pit. It was in debt when our dad died, and I've tried to claw us out of it, but you have to have money to make it. Right?" He looks tired. Maybe we had this all wrong. He's not angry—he's frustrated—exhausted.

"What were you studying before you came home to raise Sofina?" I pour us both another drink and wave the bottle at the waitress behind the bar, who nods in acknowledgment of my request.

"Art."

"Really?" I raise a brow and get a middle finger from him in response.

"I wanted to be a tattooist, not some shit one in a ten-dollar skull store, but real art. Intricate and life-changing. Not just inking skin, but creating art."

"Let me buy the bar," I say abruptly, taking him off guard.

He tenses, scowling at me. "Fuck no. You think I'd let you buy my silence so you can use my sister how you see fit with no interference from me?"

I can't help it. I laugh. He's watched too many movies or is simply fucked in the head. "You're insane. You know that, right?"

"I didn't give up my entire life to come back here to raise Sofina only to allow some pervert hanging a contract like a fish hook so she'd spread her legs for him."

My fist slams down on the table, startling him. "You're way out of line, Lucca, and should hold your fucking tongue." I roll my neck and open the new bottle the waitress placed on our table. "Sofina's contract was in place and signed before anything progressed with us. If she wanted to leave me right now, she would still have an ironclad contract that offers her all her heart could desire." I push the bottle toward him and continue. "I've never dated or had relations with an artist from our label before and I take my business very seriously. I've never had to use tactics to get women. What Sofina and I have is real. A connection I didn't expect or was looking for. It just was."

"She's too young," he snaps.

"To know she's in love? To know her own mind and make her own choices? How old were you when you fell in love?"

"It's different."

"Why? Because she's your sister?" I roll my eyes, flicking my watch on my wrist to check the time. Won't be long until she's on. "We're not that different, you and I. My mother died, and I had to be the man, take care of my younger brother, and step up. But you need to know. You did your job. She's grown. She's starting her career and her life."

"I don't know who I am without her. She's all I've got." He bows his head and places his hands in his hair.

"Then don't lose her by giving her ultimatums and expecting her to choose a mediocre life. It's beneath her. She's too talented, Lucca. Don't darken her dreams by making her live them without you."

His head snaps up, his eyes accusing. "Why do you care? Why did you call me here?"

"Because she misses you. I see her hurting, and it pains me to see her in distress."

"You act like you love her," he sneers.

"I do love her," I confirm, truthful and determined for him to understand that.

"You want my approval and for me to let you have her."

"She's already mine, Lucca. I'm not asking for anything. I'm giving you the chance to stop being a dick and give your sister what she actually needs."

"And what's that?"

"You. Your support and love."

The room becomes silent as the mic croaks and Sofina is introduced.

Nina makes her way over to us and loiters at the side of the booth we're sitting in, so I gesture for her to join us. She sits next to Lucca, her face a little pale.

"I know you from somewhere, right?" Lucca asks her with a furrowed brow.

Blushing, she shakes her head and offers a tight smile. "No, I don't think so."

I hold in a snort. *You a member of any private clubs, Lucca?*

My attention falls to the stage as I watch my girl take her place as the star she is. She glows under the spotlight like a princess. Her hands tremble as she positions the mic and takes a seat on a stool placed in front of it. My heart stills when a melody from a piano sets the tone, and then she sings. I fall deeper for the girl with the angel voice.

12

Sofina

Nerves start as wiggling caterpillars in my gut, but as soon as the music starts, they turn into butterflies and take flight, lifting me up. Singing feels natural when I close my eyes and give into it. The moment the first words tumble from my throat, it's like I need to let the rest escape in order to breathe. As I sing the lyrics, I think about the man who inspired them. Ronan. Handsome, sweet, protective Ronan.

Take care of me.

When the world is throwing rocks at me, shield me and protect me.

Hold me. Love me.

Please…just take care of me.

And I'll take care of you, too.

When I finish on a high note, my adrenaline is pumping the blood so fast through my veins I feel drunk on the feeling. The cheers ring in my ear and an uncontrollable smile takes over my face. When the stage light dims, I can see the audience and my breath stills when I see Lucca standing right there.

He moves around a table and goes to step on stage when a big security guy comes from the sideline and grabs him. Oh God. My brother is a hothead and someone grabbing him won't go over well. I need to intervene. I race forward as Lucca struggles and hits out at the man as I knew he eventually would. He and the security guard get into a scuffle that ends up involving other people.

My stomach drops when the quarrel ensues and then screams and shouts ring out. Tables are knocked over, and people are trying to move out of the way of the chaos. But it's creating more madness.

I can't get to Lucca or even see him anymore. Acid floods my bones and lead fills my shoes. Everything stills, and sounds morph and distort. I can't focus. I can't see through the mass of people. I'm being jostled around by panicked bodies.

I faintly hear my name being anxiously called,

and then two secure arms wrap around me from behind, and a familiar scent cocoons me, and the baritone of Ronan's voice penetrates the chaotic noise, and I take a breath.

He's lifting me from the floor and carrying me to the back of the stage area. I'm placed on my feet and spun to face him. Frown lines are etched into his beautiful features as he studies me and runs his hands over my body, checking me for injuries.

"My brother," I choke.

"I'll go get him. Don't move from here. Okay?"

I nod, but he doesn't move.

"I need you to say you promise."

"I promise."

The shouting and screams have silenced. A sickness settles in my stomach. The night was going so well, and it turned to shit in a heartbeat.

Police enter the club, and my knees weaken. Oh God, are we going to be arrested? Suddenly Ronan is back and not alone. A muscular cop is with him and Lucca.

I sigh in relief, but it's short-lived when I see he's got a busted lip where his ring used to be and a black eye threatening. That's not the worst of it. His hands are cuffed.

"Stop struggling, or I'll throw you in a cell for

the night, asshole," the cop growls at Lucca, manhandling him like he's made of nothing.

Tears fill my eyes and spill over. "Lucca."

His eyes find mine and darken. "I'm sorry. I only wanted to tell you how good you were."

My chest heaves and voice hitches, "Really?"

"Can we move this out the back? The manager here is pissed and wants to press charges. Luckily, he speaks the language of money like the best of us and is a friend," Ronan growls.

Once outside the cop un-cuffs Lucca and shoves him toward me.

"Stay out of trouble, punk. And don't be throwing your weight around when you're half the damn size of the other guy."

Rubbing his wrists, Lucca doesn't say anything, and I can't help myself, I'm so relieved he's okay and not in trouble I launch myself at him, and he catches me barely and lets out a wisp of air from his lungs.

"I missed you," I sob.

"I missed you too, brat."

"Thanks for doing this, Blaine," Ronan says to the cop.

"You're lucky I was working tonight," Blaine grumbles back.

"I know. I appreciate this. You're always saving my ass. When are you going to give up the blue uniform and come work for me?" Ronan jests. "I could use you to keep fuckers like Xavi in line."

I release my brother and give them my attention.

The cop is tall and muscular. Handsome with the air of authority that comes with the uniform.

"That asshole still giving you trouble? As much as I'd like to whoop that dude's arrogant ass, there's not enough action in security for me," he replies with a breathtaking grin. "You know I like the thrill of danger." He reminds me of Ronan with his commanding, daddy tone about him.

"I have to get going. Take care of your girl and call me when you need to."

They shake hands, and then Ronan is by my side, pulling me into his arms. Lucca allows him to take over the comforting and I sigh. This was a shitty way for things to go, but we're here all three of us together. That's more than I could have hoped for.

"We should get out of here," Ronan states, but Lucca doesn't move.

"Your boyfriend offered to buy the bar."

"What?" I gasp.

Ronan tightens his hold on me before saying, "It would be in your name. You'd be the owner, Sofina. You can do what you want, what you envisioned for the place, and we can bring in managers to run it for you while you're pursuing your career."

"Lucca? Is that what you want…to sell?"

Shrugging, he shakes his head. "I fucking hate the place, Sof. I only keep it for you, but I see now it's been a burden for us both."

"What will you do?"

Kicking at a stone on the ground, he barks out a laugh. It's manic and weird. "I dunno, go back to school, maybe. Go back to Boston."

"You'd go back to find her?"

"No, that's way in the past, but I could finish school, and later, open my own shop."

Emotion clogs my heart and throat, and I break down. I've been holding him back all these years. He was unhappy, and he was willing to live that way for me. We both deserve to be happy. "I'll buy you out of the bar. I have my own signing money. Let me lift the burden and give something back to you."

"Sof…"

"Please."

Grabbing me, he hugs me to him and I know everything is going to work out for us both.

"I'm sorry," Lucca mutters. "For being such an asshole."

I grin at him. "I'm sorry you're an asshole too."

"Brat."

Laughing, I playfully punch his stomach. "You raised me that way."

EPILOGUE

Ronan

Six months later…

"Cool place," Blaine says, drumming his fingers on the bar top.

I run my fingers over the countertop. Beneath the epoxy layer are thousands of blue rocks with sparkly diamond-looking gems sprinkled in between. "Her idea."

He smirks and sips his beer. "The lights?"

"All her."

"What is it exactly that you did?" he asks. "You're pretty proud for doing jack shit."

I chuckle, my eyes glued to the stage that's lit up with blue lights. "I was the moral support."

"You're so pussy-whipped."

"Better than being dick slapped."

He snorts before giving me a wicked look. "Don't knock it until you try it." His eyes track a guy wearing leather pants as he walks by. Dirty bastard.

"Hey, Roughers," a sweet voice calls out. "Thanks for coming out tonight! We have an incredible lineup on the roster. Make sure you holler at Hollie for a drink and then settle in for some amazing songs."

My girl owns the little stage in her sexy black dress and gorgeous brown curls. The V-cut of the fabric dips dangerously low, teasing me of what lies beneath. Tonight, I'll fuck that cleavage as punishment for putting it on display for every man in this place. Then, I'll paint it with my cum to remind her of who she belongs to. As though she senses my filthy thoughts, she seeks me out and smiles shyly at me.

Hollie slides another drink in front of me and winks. She's been made bar manager and is pretty fucking good at it.

Lucca fucked off back to Boston to finish school, but I get the suspicion that's not all he went back there to finish. He keeps in regular contact and that keeps my girl happy.

My eyes track back to *her*. I dip my head and flash her a wolfish grin.

She prattles on about the people on the roster while I take in the scene. The bar is crowded as fuck. It didn't take long for Ren to do his social media Twitter shit and get Diamond in the Rough a cult following with his rave reviews. Not to mention, we've signed several people since Ritz Russo's became Diamond in the Rough. That shit travels fast and now the talent list is months booked out.

"We love you, Sofina!" several girls squeal out at once. "Sing 'Take Care of Me'!"

Our song.

The song she wrote about us.

"Pussy-whipped," Blaine says with a laugh.

"Fuck off, man. You're just jealous my dick is happy."

Sofina laughs at the girls but gives them a nod. "One song."

The crowd cheers and pride surges through me. With Bastian's support, she recorded her first album, *At First Sight*, in only two months. She didn't want to tour, but with Ren's help, he was able to get her name trending on every social media site available. Sof's already a household name and has her own little bar groupies who come to see her and get shit signed. It's fucking cute to see her blush as she signs albums and posters. For someone who doesn't tour, she has some of the highest album sales already at Harose Records. Ren's trying to talk her into a small East Coast tour, but she's reluctant. When it comes to her career, I let her make her own decisions.

But the moment she steps off that stage and into my arms, she follows my rules. My girl is compliant and eager to please. And I reward her like she's never dreamed.

"This song is dedicated to my daddy," she purrs, her face burning crimson.

"Oh, Jesus," Blaine groans.

"Fuck off," I grunt, my sole focus on her.

The bar comes along with her throaty music that makes my blood buzz in my veins. She's fucking amazing. And I'm not blinded because I love her. It's the goddamn truth. I hear all the words that are words she says to me when we're alone.

Take care of me.

When the world is throwing rocks at me, shield me and protect me.

Hold me. Love me.

Please...just take care of me.

And I'll take care of you, too.

She does take care of me. Where she needs encouragement and praise and motherfucking orgasms, I need her soft smiles, sweet words, and gentle touch. My girl gives it freely and I never take that gift for granted.

Like I told her once before, we're not quite complete without the other.

But when we're together, we're fucking amazing.

As soon as she finishes, the crowd goes wild and then someone else starts singing.

"When's the wedding?" Blaine teases.

I ignore him and stand as Sofina rushes over to me. She throws her arms around my neck, kissing me in that hot, passionate way that'll get her fucked in the car before we ever make it home. Grabbing her ass, I pull her tight against me.

"You were great up there," I praise. "Such a good, good girl."

She pulls away to grin at me. "Thanks, Daddy."

I take her left hand and pull it toward Blaine. "To answer your question, asshole, the wedding's in October. Find a fuckin' suit that isn't blue."

"No fucking way," he utters in shock. "You possessive little shit."

"Nah, man," I say, turning my attention back to Sofina. "Not possessive. Just love."

But it's more than *just love* with her.

It's just…everything.

The End

WATCH ME

Up Next!

From international bestselling authors, **Ker Dukey and K Webster** *comes a **fast-paced**, hot, **instalove** standalone **lunchtime read** from their KKinky Reads collection!*

I like to watch.

It's a compulsion I can't stop.
Now my desire is centered around one woman.
My obsession borders on stalking, but the glass wall keeps me in check.

She can't see my face, yet she dances in an intensely erotic and intimate way that feels designed just for me.
She likes when I watch her.

But things are about to change when she waltzes out of that room and into my tattoo parlor, turning my world completely upside down.

And there's no glass wall this time.

*This is a steamy, kinky romance sure to make you blush! A perfect combination of sweet and sexy you can **devour in one sitting**! You'll get a **happy ending** that'll make you swoon!*

This is not a dark romance.

BOOKS BY
KER DUKEY & K WEBSTER

Pretty Little Dolls Series:
Pretty Stolen Dolls
Pretty Lost Dolls
Pretty New Doll
Pretty Broken Dolls

The V Games Series:
Vlad
Ven
Vas

KKinky Reads Collection:
Share Me
Choke Me
Daddy Me

The Elite Seven Series:
Lust by Ker Dukey
Pride by J.D. Hollyfield
Wrath by Claire C. Riley
Envy by MN Forgy
Gluttony by K Webster
Sloth by Giana Darling
Greed by Ker Dukey and K Webster

Four Fathers Series:
Blackstone by J.D. Hollyfield
Kingston by Dani Rene
Pearson by K Webster
Wheeler by Ker Dukey

Four Sons Series:
Nixon by Ker Dukey
Hayden by J.D. Hollfield
Brock by Dani Rene
Camden by K Webster

ACKNOWLEDGEMENTS

Thank you to our wonderful husbands. Baby Daddy and Mr. Webster are the real inspirations!

Ker and K would like to thank each other for being so amazing and beautiful and sweet and precious and funny and talented and hard working and… yeah, you get the point. (We love each other 1000%!)

A huge thank you to our reader groups. You all are insanely supportive and we can't thank you enough.

Thanks so much to Terrie Arasin and Misty Walker! Two of the best PAs everrrr! We love you ladies!

A gigantic thank you to those who always help K out. Elizabeth Clinton, Ella Stewart, Misty Walker, Holly Sparks, Jillian Ruize, Gina Behrends, Wendy Rinebold and Nikki Ash—you ladies are amazing!

Great thanks to Ker's awesome ladies for helping make this book is as awesome as can be! Couldn't have done it without you: Ashley Cestra, Rosa Saucedo, PA Allison, Teresa Nicholson, and KimBookJunkie.

A big thank you to our author friends who have given us your friendship and your support. You have no idea how much that means to us.

Thank you to all of our blogger friends both big and small that go above and beyond to always share our stuff. You all rock! #AllBlogsMatter

Emily A. Lawrence with Lawrence Editing, thank you SO much for editing this book. You rock!!

Thank you Stacey Blake for being amazing as always when formatting our books and in general. We love you!

A big thanks to our PR gal, Nicole Blanchard. You are fabulous at what you do!

Lastly but certainly not least of all, thank you to all of the wonderful readers out there who are willing to hear our stories and enjoy the characters like we do. It means the world to us!

ABOUT
KER DUKEY

My books all tend to be darker romance, the edge of your seat, angst-filled reads. My advice to my readers when starting one of my titles… prepare for the unexpected.

I have always had a passion for storytelling, whether it be through lyrics or bedtime stories with my sisters growing up.

My mom would always have a book in her hand when I was young and passed on her love for reading, inspiring me to venture into writing my own. Not all love stories are made from light—some are created in darkness but are just as powerful and worth telling.

When I'm not lost in the world of characters, I love spending time with my family. I'm a mom and that comes first in my life, but when I do get down time, I love attending music concerts or reading events with my younger sister.

News Letter sign up: eepurl.com/OpJxT

Website: authorkerdukey.com

Facebook: www.facebook.com/KerDukeyauthor

Twitter: twitter.com/KerDukeyauthor

Instagram: www.instagram.com/kerdukey

BookBub: www.bookbub.com/profile/ker-dukey

Goodreads: www.goodreads.com/author/show/7313508.Ker_Dukey

Contact me here:
Ker: Kerryduke34@gmail.com
Ker's PA: terriesin@gmail.com

ABOUT
K WEBSTER

K Webster is the *USA Today* bestselling author of over seventy-five romance books in many different genres including contemporary romance, historical romance, paranormal romance, dark romance, sci-fi romance, romantic suspense, taboo romance, and erotic romance. When not spending time with her hilarious and handsome husband and two adorable children, she's active on social media connecting with her readers.

Her other passions besides writing include reading and graphic design. K can always be found in front of her computer chasing her next idea and taking action. She looks forward to the day when she will see one of her titles on the big screen.

Join K Webster's newsletter to receive a couple of updates a month on new releases and exclusive content. To join, all you need to do is go here (www.authorkwebster.com).

Facebook: www.facebook.com/authorkwebster

Blog: authorkwebster.wordpress.com

Twitter: twitter.com/KristiWebster

Email: kristi@authorkwebster.com

Goodreads: www.goodreads.com/user/show/10439773-k-webster

Instagram: instagram.com/kristiwebster

KKINKY READS
COLLECTION

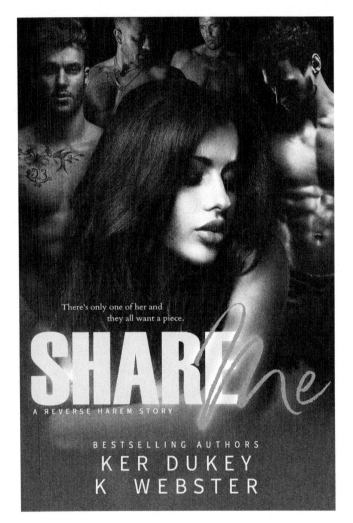

They have one job.

Keep me safe.

But none of us are safe against the allure we have when we're together.

Control and professionalism used to be something they prided themselves on.

But now that we're secluded and alone, lines blur and control quickly loses to need.

Someone is trying to snuff out my life, but they may not get the chance if I'm devoured whole by my saviors first.

This is a fiery-hot mfmmm romance sure to make you self-combust! A perfect combination of sweet and sexy with a smidgen of suspense! You'll get a happy ending that'll make you swoon!

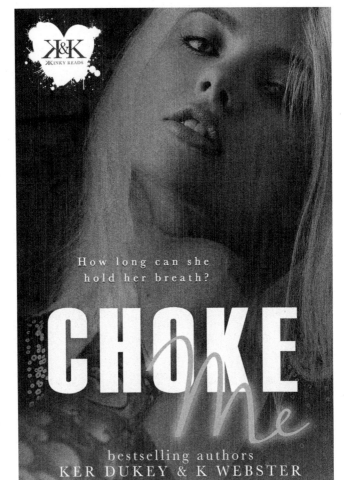

CHOKE Me

I had a plan.
Make Ren Hayes pay.
But plans don't always turn out the way we want them to.

He was found not guilty of murdering my best friend.
But that doesn't make him innocent.
In my eyes, he's guilty.

Guilty of charming everyone around him into believing his innocence.
Guilty of being so intoxicating I forget who he is—what he is.
And guilty of awakening parts of me I never knew existed before his touch.

I know eventually, I'll succumb.
His allure beckons me.
Keeping me on the edge of madness between lust and hate.

In the end, it's me who's guilty.
Guilty of allowing him to take my breath away.

This is a super steamy romance sure to take your breath away! A perfect combination of sweet and sexy with a smidgen of suspense that you can gobble up in just an hour or two! You'll get a happy ending that'll make you swoon!

Printed in Great Britain
by Amazon